USA TODAY BESTSELLING AUTHOR
NANCY WARREN

THE GREAT WITCHES BAKING SHOW

FIRST IN A NEW SERIES
OF CULINARY COZY MYSTERIES

ISBN: ebook 978-1-928145-67-7

ISBN: print 978-1-928145-69-1

Cover Design by Lou Harper of Cover Affairs

Ambleside Publishing

INTRODUCTION

A baker with secrets
Witches in trouble
The cameras are rolling
On your marks, get set, die!

Poppy Wilkinson is thrilled to be chosen as a contestant on The Great British Baking Contest. As an American with English roots, winning the crown as Britain's Best Baker would open doors she's dreamed of. In more ways than one. Appearing on the reality show is her chance to get into Broomewode Hall and uncover the secrets of her past.

But strange things are happening on the show's set: accusations of sabotage, a black cat that shadows Poppy, suspiciously unsociable residents at Broomewode Hall—and the judges can be real witches.

There are murmurs that Broomewode is an energy vortex. It certainly makes Poppy see and do things that aren't exactly normal, and seems to draw interesting characters to the neighborhood.

When a fellow contestant dies in mysterious circumstances, Poppy has more to worry about than burned pies and cakes that won't rise. There's a murderer on the loose and it's up to Poppy and her new friends to solve the crime before it becomes a real show-stopper.

From USA Today Bestselling Author Nancy Warren, this delicious series of cozy paranormal mysteries will have you guessing until the end. Includes recipes.

First in a delicious new series of culinary cozy mysteries!

The best way to keep up with new releases and special offers is to join Nancy's newsletter at **nancywarren.net.**

PRAISE FOR THE GREAT WITCHES
BAKING SHOW

"I loved it! I could not put it down once I'd started it."

— GATORFAN, AMAZON TOP 500
REVIEWER

"The characters are wonderful. More, please!"

— BARB, GOODREADS REVIEWER

"This book was funny, sweet and had a good amount of mystery and suspense which kept me invested throughout. I cannot wait to read the next book in this series."

— ERIN, GOODREADS REVIEWER

THE GREAT WITCHES BAKING SHOW

*E*lspeth Peach could not have conjured a more beautiful day. Broomewode Hall glowed in the spring sunshine. The golden Cotswolds stone manor house was a Georgian masterpiece, and its symmetrical windows winked at her as though it knew her secrets and promised to keep them. Green lawns stretched their arms wide, and an ornamental lake seemed to welcome the swans floating serene and elegant on its surface.

But if she shifted her gaze just an inch to the left, the sense of peace and tranquility broke into a million pieces. Trucks and trailers had invaded the grounds, large tents were already in place, and she could see electricians and carpenters and painters at work on the twelve cooking stations. As the star judge of the wildly popular TV series *The Great British Baking Contest,* Elspeth Peach liked to cast her discerning eye over the setup to make sure that everything was perfect.

When the reality show became a hit, Elspeth Peach had been rocketed to a household name. She'd have been just as happy to be left alone in relative obscurity, writing cookbooks and devising new recipes. When she'd first agreed to judge amateur bakers, she'd imagined a tiny production watched only by serious foodies, and with a limited run. Had she known the show would become an international success, she never would have agreed to become so public a figure. Because Elspeth Peach had an important secret to keep. She was an excellent baker, but she was an even better witch.

Elspeth had made a foolish mistake. Baking made her happy, and she wanted to spread some of that joy to others. But she never envisaged how popular the series would become or how closely she'd be scrutinized by The British Witches Council, the governing body of witches in the UK. The council wielded great power, and any witch who didn't follow the rules was punished.

When she'd been unknown, she'd been able to fudge the borders of rule-following a bit. She always obeyed the main tenet of a white witch—do no harm. However, she wasn't so good at the dictates about not interfering with mortals without good reason. Now, she knew she was being watched very carefully, and she'd have to be vigilant. Still, as nervous as she was about her own position, she was more worried about her brand-new co-host.

Jonathon Pine was another famous British baker. His cookbooks rivaled hers in popularity and sales, so it shouldn't have been a surprise that he'd been chosen as her co-judge. Except that Jonathon was also a witch.

She'd argued passionately against the council's decision to have him as her co-judge, but it was no good. She was stuck with him. And that put the only cloud in the blue sky of this lovely day.

To her surprise, she saw Jonathon approaching her. She'd imagined he'd be the type to turn up a minute before cameras began rolling. He was an attractive man of about fifty with sparkling blue eyes and thick, dark hair. However, at this moment he looked sheepish, more like a sulky boy than a baking celebrity. Her innate empathy led her to get right to the issue that was obviously bothering him, and since she was at least twenty years his senior, she said in a motherly tone, "Has somebody been a naughty witch?"

He met her gaze then. "You know I have. I'm sorry, Elspeth. The council says I have to do this show." He poked at a stone with the toe of his signature cowboy boot—one of his affectations, along with the blue shirts he always wore to bring out the color of his admittedly very pretty eyes.

"But how are you going to manage it?"

"I'm hoping you'll help me."

She shook her head at him. "Five best-selling books and a consultant to how many bakeries and restaurants? What were you thinking?"

He jutted out his bottom lip. "It started as a bit of a lark, but things got out of control. I became addicted to the fame."

"But you know we're not allowed to use our magic for personal gain."

He'd dug out the stone now with the toe of his boot, and his attention dropped to the divot he'd made in the lawn. "I know, I know. It all started innocently enough. This woman I met said no man can bake a proper scone. Well, I decided to show her that wasn't true by baking her the best scone she'd ever tasted. All right, I used a spell, since I couldn't bake a scone or anything else, for that matter. But it was a matter of principle. And then one thing led to another."

"Tell me the truth, Jonathon. Can you bake at all? Without using magic, I mean."

A worm crawled lazily across the exposed dirt, and he followed its path. She found herself watching the slow, curling brown body too, hoping. Finally, he admitted, "I can't boil water."

She could see that the council had come up with the perfect punishment for him by making the man who couldn't bake a celebrity judge. He was going to be publicly humiliated. But, unfortunately, so was she.

He groaned. "If only I'd said no to that first book deal. That's when the real trouble started."

Privately, she thought it was when he magicked a scone into being. It was too easy to become addicted to praise and far too easy to slip into inappropriate uses of magic. One bad move could snowball into catastrophe. And now look where they were.

When he raised his blue eyes to meet hers, he looked quite desperate. "The council told me I had to learn how to bake and come and do this show without using any magic at all." He sighed. "Or else."

"Or else?" Her eyes squinted as though the sun were blinding her, but really she dreaded the answer.

He lowered his voice. "Banishment."

She took a sharp breath. "As bad as that?"

He nodded. "And you're not entirely innocent either, you know. They told me you've been handing out your magic like it's warm milk and cuddles. You've got to stop, Elspeth, or it's banishment for you, too."

She swallowed. Her heart pounded. She couldn't believe the council had sent her a message via Jonathon rather than calling her in themselves. She'd never used her magic for personal gain, as Jonathon had. She simply couldn't bear to see these poor, helpless amateur bakers blunder when she could help. They were so sweet and eager. She became attached to them all. So sometimes she turned on an oven if a baker forgot or saved the biscuits from burning, the custard from curdling. She'd thought no one had noticed.

However, she had steel in her as well as warm milk, and she spoke quite sternly to her new co-host. "Then we must make absolutely certain that nothing goes wrong this season. You will practice every recipe before the show. Learn what makes a good crumpet, loaf of bread and Victoria sponge. You will study harder than you ever have in your life, Jonathon. I will help you where I can, but I won't go down with you."

He leveled her with an equally steely gaze. "All right. And you won't interfere. If some show contestant forgets to turn their oven on, you don't make it happen by magic."

Oh dear. So they *did* know all about her little intervention in Season Two.

"And if somebody's caramelized sugar starts to burn, you do not save it."

Oh dear. And that.

"Fine. I will let them flail and fail, poor dears."

"And I'll learn enough to get by. We'll manage, Elspeth."

The word banishment floated in the air between them like the soft breeze.

"We'll have to."

*a*s life-changing moments go, getting the call that I'd been chosen to compete in *The Great British Baking Contest* was right up there. I'd practiced, auditioned and practiced some more. I was a decent home baker, but was I really the best in Britain? Probably not. But I didn't have to be.

The contest was my way of getting into Broomewode Hall, where the show was filmed. I had my own reasons for going there that had nothing to do with baking.

Still, it hadn't been easy to be chosen. There were thousands of applicants every year and then an excruciating selection process, where the show's producers chose twelve from the short list and made us bake on camera. Some people went to pieces; some were just really boring. They randomly selected bakers off the short list and tried out different combinations of personalities, a bit like baking, really, seeing which ingredients created the most interesting results. I quickly learned that the trick was to be a good character, try to be funny, be a good sport, pretend you didn't notice that cameras were on you and a clock was ticking down the minutes, and still turn out a decent jam tart.

Easy peasy! *Not.*

One of the reasons they chose me for the show, I think, was that while I was British, I'd grown up in the States, which was kind of fun, as the show had become a huge hit in America. I'd also started life in a bakery. Or, more accurately, in a cardboard box outside a bakery in Norton St. Philip, a charming village near Bath in Somerset.

I like to think my mother, whoever she was, chose the bakery so she knew I'd be warm and, since bakers start work so early, I'd be found. And I was. When Gareth Philpott came to work that morning, he said he looked into the box and found me wide-awake, staring up at him. Not crying, not fussing, just staring as though I'd expected him. They named me Poppy. The Philpotts would have kept me if they could have. They're a nice family, but they already had three children, and the authorities don't just give a family a baby because they happened to stumble across one. First they tried to find my mother or any information at all about my origins. When that proved impossible, I was adopted by Agatha and Leland Wilkinson, and they became my parents.

They were both teachers. They'd tried for years to have their own children, and their delight in getting me was reflected in the way they pretty much turned their lives around to give me the best upbringing they could. They were loving parents, kind and patient. Strict when they had to be. We lived in Bath for the first eight years of my life, and then my dad was offered a teaching job in Seattle.

I grew up there, mostly, lost the British accent, became a typical American teenager, and then when I finished high school, my folks retired and moved back to the UK. I could have stayed in Seattle. I had friends, and I could've gone to college there, but I chose to come back to England. I think, deep down, it's always felt like home. Besides, like a lot of adopted kids, the mystery of my beginnings haunts me.

Soon after returning to England, my folks moved to the south of France to bask in warmer weather, grow lavender and cook gourmet meals. My dad, who taught history, was writing a book. My mom was learning French.

They'd saved up a nice chunk of change for me to go to college but, in spite of having teachers as parents, I never felt the urge. I was always more artistic than intellectual, so I went to an art and design college for two years, and they let me use the rest of the money toward buying a tiny cottage in Norton St. Philip. It's probably crazy, and nobody even thinks my mother was from there, but I started my life in that village and so it pulled me back. The Philpotts still ran the bakery and were my second family. I guess you'll always have a bond with the person who picked you up off the street as a newborn. Besides, growing up as an only child, I was fascinated by their sprawling, noisy family.

I became a freelance graphic designer, which allowed me to work from home. Yes, it could be lonely, but it was easier to hide my condition. I don't know what else to call it.

I see people who aren't really there.

When I was little, I was often visited by a boy about my own age. He was kind of bossy and talked funny, but he was my playmate. He told me his name was Peter. When my parents found out about Peter they took me to a child psychologist, and everyone determined that I had an imaginary friend, perfectly common in only children.

Good thing I never told anyone that Peter wore strange clothes. Not until much later, when I was researching the history of the Pacific Northwest for a high school essay, did I see pictures of that same clothing. Peter wore a beaver-skin cap, a double-breasted wool coat with brass buttons and leather boots. His hair hung to his shoulders. I found a boy who looked very much like him in a photo dated 1858. By then, I'd learned to be a lot more careful about the strange people I came across. I learned not to react to seeing people when I entered a room or a house until someone else mentioned them, in case they were ghosts. I know it sounds super strange, but you get used to it, and I've never felt scared. In fact, I have a lot to be thankful to ghosts for. They've taught me to be open-minded, treat strangers with kindness, and that the decisions we make in life have consequences.

Working from home meant not having to be on my guard all the time. Probably, when I bought my cottage, I should have chosen something brand-new, where no one had yet died. But when I first glimpsed The Olde Bakery, I fell for the low stone walls, the rambling herb garden and the kitchen, which combined flagstone floors, an original fireplace and modern appliances. I was often visited by a woman wearing an old-fashioned dress and apron and a mob cap. Her name was Mildred, and she used to be the cook there. She shared all of her secret baking tips with me, although obviously she wasn't much good as a taste tester. Sometimes a man paced up and down outside, but if I opened the door and invited him in, he disappeared.

Even though these people were ghosts, we got along. Mildred often scolded me though, criticizing my cooking skills and offering me advice. She pretended to be appalled at all the modern conveniences, like the blender, food processor and microwave, but secretly I thought she was jealous they didn't have them in her time. I spent hours baking, practicing to get on the show, and so with no one at home to give me an honest opinion, I packed my baked goods up and headed to the Philpotts' house. It was much newer than mine, being built in the last hundred years.

Gina Philpott was my age and my best friend. We'd been joined at the hip since we were little, and she would make me sit still for hours while she crimped my hair and painted my face with her mum's makeup. Even though I was away for fifteen years, we'd stayed in touch, visiting whenever our family made the trip back to the UK, and remained close. She was a hairstylist and makeup artist now and worked on *The Great British Baking Contest*. She'd helped me with my application and even did my makeup and hair before the first on-camera audition. She was also the only one who knew why I really wanted to get on that show.

It went all the way back to when I was just a baby in that cardboard box. After the police finished trying to trace my birth mother, they gave the items to my mom and dad. The box had contained me, obviously, wearing a terry-towel onesie from Marks & Spencer. However, without an actual date of purchase or any clue as to who did the buying, it was impossible to track down which Marks & Spencer had sold the item or to whom. Ditto the disposable diaper. The box was a Somerset apple box, and inside it, I was wrapped snuggly in a blanket. The apple box was common enough and yielded no clues but a faint smell of apples.

The blanket was more interesting. It was made of wool in

greens and blues with a hint of red in a curious pattern. The police couldn't trace where it might have been bought from, or the wool, and decided it must have been knitted by hand. It was exquisite work. I couldn't imagine having the time, patience or skill to knit something so fine.

There was no note in the box, no locket broken in half so I might one day find my birth mother, who'd have the other half. The only clue to where I came from was that blanket.

I kept it draped casually over a chair in my little living room. Too small for a bed, it was a pretty throw and the only link I had with my birth family. Probably because I saw it every day and knew its pattern so intimately, I recognized it immediately when I saw it again.

I saw my baby blanket one day when I was watching *The Great British Baking Contest.* They always filmed at Broomewode Hall, a Georgian manor house that wasn't open to the public. Broomewode Hall was the seat of the Earl of Frome, Robert Champney and his family. The Champneys made money by letting their estate be used for the show and doing weddings, the way a lot of those old British aristocrats did to make ends meet. During one of the behind-the-scenes segments on the show, Lady Frome showed them around her home.

As the camera panned around the great dining hall and Lady Frome described the paintings, I was instantly trans-fixed by a woman in an oil painting who seemed to be wearing my baby blanket! I saw now that, in fact, it was a shawl. But the pattern was the same. I was certain of it.

And from that very moment, I began my quest to find out more about Broomewode Hall. Lord and Lady Frome guarded their privacy tenaciously, and it was impossible to get access to them and their family home. Besides, what would I say? "I think one of your ancestors once wore my baby blanket? The best way I could think of to spend time there was to qualify as a baker on *The Great British Baking Contest.*

I'd done it. Against incredible odds, I'd been chosen as one of twelve bakers. It was one step toward finding out who I really was. All I had to do now was figure out how to get the rest of the way.

CHAPTER 2

$\mathcal{I}$t was a beautiful April day. Sunlight dappled across the pale green leaves and new shoots, while daffodils and tulips stood like royalty on top of a carpet of bluebells. It was the perfect weather for our first day of filming. The famous tents stretched across the green lawn in front of me. I was so nervous, I wanted to turn around, run back home and throw up. I hadn't thought this through. People I knew and millions of strangers would watch me cooking on television. I was terrified of making a massive fool of myself. Maybe they wouldn't even wait until the end of the first episode, but chuck me off the show after I failed to master some British baking delicacy I'd never heard of.

My brain was so addled, I didn't think I'd be able to tell the difference between a wooden spoon and a Bundt pan. Everything I'd ever known or thought I knew about baking slipped right out of my head. It was as though someone had taken my carefully collected file of recipes and turned it upside down over a trash can.

I stole nervous glances at the other contestants gathered

on the lawn for our pre-filming pep talk. None of them looked nearly as nervous as me. They looked like bakers. Professional. Confident. Experienced. Their brains filled with old and original family recipes, their arm muscles honed by years of beating egg whites by hand, fashioning marzipan animals and kneading their own bread—no doubt from the grain grown on their own farms and allotments.

I was such a lightweight by comparison, I was bound to be the first one voted off the show. What had I been thinking? At least Gina had done my hair and makeup for the show earlier that morning and helped me choose my outfit for today. She'd styled my long, dark hair in loose curls and used powders and potions to make my hazel eyes stand out. I was wearing a purple cotton blouse over jeans. She said it would look good on camera and flatter my complexion. If I was going to embarrass myself on international TV, then at least I'd look my best while doing it.

We were an assorted bunch—of different ages and backgrounds. A grandmotherly type smiled at me as though she could see how scared I was. I knew from the information package we'd been given that her name was Maggie Wheelan and she had five grandchildren. She must have been baking long before I was even born and so had decades more experience. Her glance passed on from me, as she no doubt dismissed me as competition.

A male voice beside me said, "You look like you're trying to remember how to turn an oven knob to the on position."

I laughed. "Right now I can't even remember what an oven is."

The speaker was a bit older than me, probably in his early thirties, and wore a red shirt patterned with cars and trucks. His red hair was spiky, and his green eyes twinkled as though he wasn't taking any of this seriously.

I wasn't fooled. Every one of us here had worked our butts off to make it this far. We were all hoping to be crowned Britain's Best Baker.

As though he'd followed my train of thought, he said, "I just hope I'm not the first one voted off."

"Me too. Anything but that."

He grinned at me. "Well, we can't both be voted off first, so let's be friends instead. Then, if one of us goes, the other can bang on to the TV cameras about what a great person we were, maybe squeeze out a crocodile tear or two."

I laughed. "Deal."

He held out his hand. "I'm Gerald Parterre, but everyone calls me Gerry."

"I'm Poppy Wilkinson."

We'd already been told a little about our fellow contestants. What I knew about Gerry was that he was a home renovation specialist who'd been baking since he was a child. When he finished a customer's renovation, he always baked them a cake to celebrate. I thought he sounded nice and was thankful to find a friendly face.

"You must be the youngest," he said to me, then leaned in. "Also the prettiest."

"I'm twenty-five," I told him and ignored the rest of his comment. I was the girl-next-door type and knew it. The prettiest woman on the show was undoubtedly Florence Cinelli. She was film-star gorgeous with a mane of reddish-brown hair, wide-set eyes and a generous mouth enhanced by flawless makeup. Her clothes could have been featured on a runway in Milan. She made me feel that five minutes in the morning with toothbrush, hairbrush and washcloth wasn't enough of a beauty routine. I was too intimidated to do more than just nod in her direction. How did she keep her red nails so pristine while baking? She wore a cherry-red dress that showed off gorgeous legs and high heels. How was she going to bake in heels?

Maggie, the grandmother, began going around and introducing herself to everyone, and we all followed her lead. I could barely remember my own name, but I tried to concentrate as I shook hands with Gaurav, a research scientist who'd just returned from visiting his family in India and found the weather chilly. I told him he'd soon warm up when the ovens were going.

Evie was a bit older, fiftyish, I supposed. She was an administrator for the NHS and told me she liked to bring in spices from Jamaica, where she'd been born.

Hamish MacDonald was a Scottish police officer. He looked tough and no-nonsense and then melted my heart when he admitted his specialty was his granny's shortbread recipe. He lived near Fort William and raised Shetland ponies.

There wasn't time for more. Donald Friesen, the series producer, approached, and with him were the big stars of the show, Elspeth Peach and Jonathon Pine. I got such a thrill seeing the two star bakers. As you do with celebrities, I felt as though I knew them. Then Elspeth turned her gaze to me and smiled as though she knew me, too. She gave a tiny nod, and I felt a shiver run down my back.

"Attention, everyone, please." Donald Friesen was intense and energetic. I knew from Gina that he'd just turned forty and was an ambitious company man. Being series producer to the baking contest was his life. He had short black hair and wore a snappy teal suit and shiny black loafers. He reminded us to be ourselves, forget all about the cameras that would follow us around, and act naturally. Yeah, right, like it was going to be that easy. "It's meant to be fun!" he said. "So focus only on your workstation and whatever you're baking."

Although this was a competition, they didn't want us to appear to be competitive. It reminded me a little bit of a yoga teacher who had once said yoga was all about you and your mat. As though people weren't peeking at the other yogis, seeing who could stretch further, hold the pose longer or who looked better in their skintight yoga gear. If people were competitive at yoga class, I couldn't imagine how bad it would get on a televised contest.

"Oh, and don't forget that all of you will be mic'd," he continued. "So you might want to remember to take it off when you go to the bathroom and try not to say things you wouldn't want the sound guy to overhear." There was nervous laughter from all of us. Donald smiled, and I saw for the first time how his pale skin was pockmarked around his chin and mouth.

The tent where we'd be filming was a vast expanse of crisp white calico erected across the gorgeous green lawns of the estate. Its floor was laid with long planks of polished pine, where I hoped I wouldn't drop my cake with nervousness. It's hard to explain what it's like to step into that tent knowing that more than a million people will end up watching you baking under pressure while trying to keep your cool, remember your recipe, look like you know what you're doing, and pretend you aren't terrified that you're going to be the next one sent home. Let's just say that my stomach was in knots and my hands were clammy with sweat.

Donald called over the hosts and judges and introduced them. There was a shiver of excitement as Elspeth Peach and Jonathon Pine came forward to meet us all. They were huge celebrities, and they'd be deciding who stayed and who went in the weeks ahead. Up close, Elspeth Peach seemed as perfectly put-together and as genuinely nice as she did on TV. "It's so wonderful to see someone so young who is so accomplished at baking," she said to me. I thanked her and said, "I hope I hold up under pressure."

"You'll be fine," she said. Then she held out her hand. As I shook it, a feeling like an electric shock went up my arm. She'd been about to move on, but she turned back and stared at me, still hanging on to my hand, which felt hot. "Are you a...?" Then she shook her head and laughed. "No. Of course, you're not." She finally let go of my hand and spoke to Gerry.

That was strange. I wondered how that sentence would have ended. But I had no time to think about the bizarre interlude as I realized that one of the two comedian hosts was reminding me that I was American. They were called Jilly and Arty, perfect comedians' names. No doubt they'd use that as the basis of little jokes as the show progressed. I'd better get used to it.

Jilly had been in a hit comedy show a decade or so ago. She had a mass of red curls and square blue glasses, but behind the lenses, her eyes looked sad.

I knew, again from Gina, that Donald had recruited Arty, as he was so popular with the younger demographic. He'd begun in stand-up and had co-written and starred in a quirky TV comedy that became a hit. He had long blond hair, big blue eyes and, Gina said, was famous for flirting with everyone.

My workstation was on the left-hand side about halfway down. I walked up to it feeling as though it were the first day of school. Blood was pounding in my ears. I was finding it hard to swallow. The counter was pristine, my supplies neatly labeled and arranged, pencils sharpened and waiting to be used. Everything was yet to come. I just hoped that I could take the pressure.

A man I hadn't seen before walked toward me. "Name's Gordon," he said. "I'm your sound guy."

I nodded a nervous hello. He tested my mic and twiddled with some wires. "Nice to meet you," I finally managed. "I guess you're the one who'll overhear me say embarrassing things. I'll try my best to keep it together." Gordon was a pleasant-looking guy. Somewhere in his thirties, he had a nice face, brownish-blond hair, blue eyes and a close-cropped beard.

"How you feeling?"

"Well, I can barely string a sentence together, let alone a cake."

"You'll be fine. The camera loves a pretty face. You've nothing to worry about." Now that he'd finished adjusting the mic, he patted my arm and moved on. Gina was running around doing final touches to makeup and hair. As Gordon walked away, she said, "Ooh, I think Gordon likes you. Look how long he spent talking to you."

I put my hand over my mic. Already there were things I didn't want Gordon to hear, and I'd only been mic'd up for five seconds. "Stop it. I'm not a man-magnet."

"Well, not usually," Gina agreed. "But I've just done your

hair and makeup. And I, Pops," she said, leaning in, "am an artist."

"The real man magnet is Florence Cinella," I said, motioning with my head to where the gorgeous Florence was currently surrounded by Arty the comedian; Donald Friesen, the series producer; Gerry, who'd promised to be my friend; Gaurav; and Hamish.

"True. I'd offer to touch up her makeup, but it would be like taking a crayon to the Mona Lisa."

"You're so good for my confidence."

Gina laughed. "You'll be fine. Keep your cool and don't panic. After the first challenge, it will get easier."

The director, a woman named Fiona, marshaled everyone to their places, and the moment we'd all hoped for arrived.

The four hosts lined up at the front of the tent. As anyone who's watched one of these programs knows, there are always two comic relief characters and then two master bakers. Elspeth Peach was well into her seventies and an absolute legend. She was known to be kind but thorough. Jonathon Pine was going to be the tough guy of the two. We'd been warned he could smash a contestant down like an under-cooked soufflé with only a word or two.

We'd already been given the first challenge ahead of time so that we could order our ingredients and have a chance to practice. Still, there's no pressure like trying to cook something with an oven you're not familiar with and mixers and pans and tools that are not your own. As any cook will tell you, equipment and utensils all have their own unique personalities. Some need a little bit of extra love and encouragement to work the way you want them to; others are stubborn, and you need to adjust to their set speed or temperature. It takes time and patience to get to know your tools. And here we were, presented with brand-new equipment. I imagined if I lasted long enough, they would become like old friends, but at the moment, we'd barely even been introduced, and I certainly didn't trust them to do my bidding. And yet, I had no choice. I'd have to put my faith in them.

I stood by my station, trying to control my shaking hands, and took a little peek at the eleven other contestants. We were a good mixed bunch of ages and backgrounds, and I knew from the contestant pack that we did a wide range of jobs too. I'd get to know them all—if I made it through the day, that is.

Jonathon Pine stepped forward. "Bakers, your first challenge will be a technical one. We want to see a perfectly airy sponge cake, and we want it to be something that could feature in a fairy tale or children's story. We're looking for interesting flavors and some artistic imagination. You have two hours. Your time starts now."

Naturally, I'd run to my best friend, Gina, when I first discovered what this challenge was going to be in hopes of learning from her stylist's artistic eye. She wanted me to do Sleeping Beauty, but that seemed too obvious. Besides, I wanted to make use of my American heritage. "Pocahontas?" she suggested doubtfully. I shook my head. We discussed ideas for ages, but it was my father, on the phone from Nice, who suggested Persephone.

My dad loved the mythical legends of Ancient Greece and Rome, and the story of Persephone was one of his favorites. Persephone was a beautiful young woman, the daughter of loving Demeter, the goddess of earth's fertility and harvest, and Zeus, the king of all the Olympians. Persephone lived a happy, fruitful life when Hades, the god of the underworld, captured her and took her to Hell to be his wife. Her mother searched everywhere for her daughter and was so upset to have lost her that she turned the earth to winter. The gods forced Hades to bring Persephone back to the earth. If she hadn't eaten anything when imprisoned, she'd be allowed to return to her mother, but Persephone had eaten a few juicy pomegranate seeds, and so the gods judged that she could only return to her mother and live above ground for half the year and spend the remaining half with Hades.

I thought this was a perfect story for a cake. It was a good talking point and allowed me to create summer on one side of the cake and winter on the other. Pomegranate would make for a gorgeous pink sponge. I just hoped I'd get the balance of bitterness and sweetness just right. And that I'd been inventive enough.

I began weighing out my ingredients, keeping my eye glued to the electric scales. Even a few ounces over or under could make all the difference. I was determined not to make any silly mistakes. It's bad enough trying to make a cake under that kind of pressure, but to add a sprinkling of extra torture, the judges and comedians wandered around and joked with the contestants. This was a big part of what made the show fun as a viewer and absolutely terrifying as a contestant. Jonathon and Elspeth were heading my way, with Jilly in tow. The camera edged closer. I sifted my flour with renewed vigor.

"I understand you're going to flavor your filling with pomegranate," Jonathon said. Was he frowning? Had I been too clever? No doubt I had. Still, Maggie had chosen Sleeping Beauty, so at least I was original.

"Yes," I replied. "I was inspired by the myth of Persephone, who was kidnapped by Hades." I explained the story, trying to remember what I'd practiced in my head and keep my voice from shaking.

"Goodness me!" exclaimed Jilly. "That's like the worst diet ever, being sent to hell for snacking on a few pomegranate seeds."

Everyone laughed, and I tried to join in, but inside I was a wreck. I was working hard to present the world of winter moving into a world rich with spring and summer in a sponge cake. In. A. Sponge. Cake.

I began to crack my eggs, but my hands were slippery with sweat. Almost in slow motion, I felt one egg slide from my grip. Oh no, I was about to drop an egg in front of the judges and on national TV. But just as I watched it tumble to the ground, Elspeth leaned forward and caught it.

"Gotcha!" she exclaimed and calmly handed me back the egg.

"Thank you," I managed to stutter.

"Phew, that was close," Jonathon said and laughed, but where the camera couldn't see, he glared at his co-host. "Lucky for you, Elspeth has lightning reflexes."

Elspeth looked stricken as though she'd done something wrong. Maybe they weren't supposed to help us poor contestants even to stop an egg from smashing to the ground. I wiped my hands on my apron. I needed to get a grip. Literally.

"Yes, you wouldn't know it, but Elspeth is a black belt in Judo," Jilly joked.

The two judges moved on, but I sensed that Jilly remained behind. *Don't look at the camera*, I reminded myself.

I knew I was blushing hard. I had the mixer going, and I was adding sugar into the eggs as they were beating. "It's quite a process, isn't it?" Jilly said. "A lot of people reckon sponge is easy, but it's much more complicated than they think." Arty joined us, and I worried that he'd start making fun of me. Of the two comedians, his tongue was sharpest.

"Yes," I said. "The secret to sponge is incorporating enough air to give a lightness to the texture, which you do by beating the eggs. But then you have to be careful not to over-cook it or undercook it, or you'll ruin all your good work by making it either too dry or too heavy." As I heard the words echo in my head, I cringed. Who did I think I was? Telling anyone how to make a sponge. But we were encouraged to do that kind of thing, to throw out little hints for the home cook. Presumably, if my sponge turned out to be a complete disaster, the viewers wouldn't listen to my tips anyway.

"Not too dry, not too wet, not too heavy. Sounds like me ordering a martini," Arty said to the camera.

Jilly smiled at me before leaving with Arty to speak to my neighbor baker, Florence Cinelli, the film-star gorgeous one. Jonathon certainly seemed to enjoy her company. "And you're a drama student?" he asked, as though it was her schooling that interested him.

"Yes. In London. I love cooking for my flatmates." She looked so glamorous and in control as she beamed at Jilly. I heard her talking about her antics as a film student and laughing a rich, warm laugh. She was an excellent storyteller, and I was sure the viewers at home would find her charming. I stole another quick peek at the other contestants. They all seemed perfectly calm and collected, like they knew exactly what they were doing. Gerry caught my eye and smiled. I rolled my eyes. I had to focus on the monumental and over-complicated task I'd set for myself. Sweat prickled the back of my neck under my hair. I knew I had to work faster.

Then I heard a cry of distress and turned to see Evie dumping her batter into the garbage. Naturally, the camera was taking it all in for the home viewer. She wailed, "I forgot the bloody sugar. I put the batter in the tins and then I turned around and saw the sugar sitting there. I'll have to start all over again."

The cameras edged closer to Evie. The production manager said, "Sorry, lovely, can you just repeat that last line for the viewers but take the swear word out of it?"

She grimaced.

Okay, so I wasn't the only one feeling the pressure. I felt sorry for Evie, as I knew the viewers loved to see this kind of silly mistake. But I was also so glad it wasn't me who'd forgotten the sugar. Not yet, anyway. Evie looked as though she might cry, and Maggie, the grandmotherly one, leaned over and said to her, "You've still got plenty of time. Take a deep breath and begin again." She was so nice.

The next hour passed in a blur, all my concentration poured into remembering each ingredient, each step of the recipe. I tried to ignore the cameras as they zoomed in on me as I placed the mixture into the oven. It was a rule. We had to have a camera filming every time we put anything into the oven or took it out. Once the door was shut on my cake, I stood for a moment, watching my tins, wishing them well. I had to laugh at myself, but I always wished my baking well.

Finally, the huge sponges I'd labored over were ready to come out of the oven. They were golden brown. Perfect. I heaved a sigh of relief. I took the marzipan I'd made earlier out of the fridge and began to roll it out. I'd practiced manipulating its soft texture into brown trees and dry grass for the autumn side of my cake, and using food coloring to turn it into green, pink, and purple blossoms for spring. I knew I didn't have time to fashion individual flowers, so I was going for sort of an Impressionist style. I hoped the judges would understand and not think I'd just made a mess of it.

When Arty called out, "Five minutes, bakers," I wanted to scream with fear and frustration. How could there only be five minutes left? I'd made just one tiny rose when I'd planned to make six. Well, there was nothing I could do about it now. I spread the thick pomegranate buttercream across the golden sponge, taking care to keep the sides neat and tidy, and assembled the marzipan trees and single flower across its peaks.

The clanger went off, signaling the end of the first round. I realized I'd been holding my breath. I stood back from the table and surveyed my work. Not bad, I thought. Not bad. My cake wasn't perfect, but I knew it was passable. Now I had a moment to see what the others had done. Every single contestant looked worried. But when I took a closer look at Gerry, he was absolutely gray. I followed his gaze to his cake and soon understood why: the middle had all but collapsed. He looked up and caught my eye. "It's not bloody cooked in the middle!" he exclaimed. But it was time to take our cakes to the front table to be judged. I gripped mine like I was holding a newborn baby, terrified in case it fell from my sweaty clutches. I'd seen that happen before.

We watched as Elspeth and Jonathon each took a forkful of the sponges. It was excruciating. I knew they were making comments about the texture and presentation, but I couldn't focus on the words. When they got to my cake, I heard buzzing in my ears. One day, I'd tune into the program and find out what they'd said. I eventually tuned back in and heard the judges saying my cake was airy and light with just the right amount of sweet bitterness from the pomegranate buttercream. I breathed out a huge sigh of relief. They didn't hate it.

They had plenty of brilliant things to say about the crumbly softness of some of the other contestants' sponges and a few sharp words of criticism too. Elspeth seemed really sorry when she shook her head over Gaurav's sponge. "Overbaked. I'm afraid it's rather dry." She turned to Jonathon, who agreed. "Yes. Definitely dry. I'm afraid you've overbaked your sponge. Decorations were good, though. I liked the reggae band. A Day of the Dead theme was a good choice."

Two contestants who seemed to have made an unlikely alliance, retired beekeeper Euan and hairdresser Priscilla, were both almost gripping onto each other as they were being judged. "Very nice texture," Jonathon said of the beekeeper.

"Perfectly pleasant," said Elspeth of Priscilla's cake.

The police officer named Hamish, who'd told the cameras he baked to deal with the stress of his job, received high praise from Jonathon, but Elspeth was a little less forthcoming. But thankfully the judging was soon over. To my huge relief, my cake came fourth, which I was pretty pleased about. I didn't expect to even come close to the top five so early on in the show.

The sweet grandmother, Maggie, who'd smiled at me earlier, took first place. She'd made some beautiful sugar flowers for her sponge; I was in awe. Maggie beamed as she was told she'd won, moving her gold-rimmed glasses from their chain around her neck onto her nose as if she couldn't believe the news. She seemed like such a lovely lady. Gerry's was the second from last. Fortunately for him, Evie never recovered from the sugar disaster. She came in at the bottom.

We barely had time to recuperate from that ordeal before we were told to tidy up everything up before lunch, after which the day's final challenge would be set.

While we tidied and prepared for the next round, Gerry was inspecting his oven. I walked over. "Never mind," I said. "We're all still getting to know our equipment. You'll do better this afternoon. At least you weren't last!"

He looked up, red-faced and fuming. "My oven's no good. I'm telling you, I set it to the correct temperature. I've made that sponge hundreds of times. There's something wrong with my oven. And I'm going to do something about it."

Gerry called over the show's electrician, Aaron Keel. He was a tough-looking guy with a shaved head and an anchor tattoo on his beefy arm. He took out a flashlight, looked into the oven's depths and began to tinker about in there. "I can't find anything wrong," he said to Gerry. "It's working perfectly."

"That can't be true!"

"Listen, mate, we test the ovens every morning. Did you notice that lovely smell as you walked in today? The crew bakes a Victoria Sponge every morning in every oven to make sure they are working perfectly."

"There's nothing worse than a poor loser," said a man walking by. He was another contestant, Marcus Hoare. I'd chatted with Marcus when all the contestants were first introduced. He was a banker from London, and I didn't warm to him at all. His crisp white shirt was buttoned all the way to the top, collar stiff with starch. His short blond hair was combed back into a single glossy wave with Brylcreem. He had a serious face and a long nose, on top of which small, round black glasses sat. In short, he was pompous and uptight, and this came across in the ordered decoration of his cake, its neat sections and surgical precision.

"That was so mean," I said as Marcus walked away.

Gerry stared after him, first in surprise, then with growing awareness. "I know him."

"You do?"

He shrugged. "I'm a contractor. I'm in and out of a lot of houses. I renovated his kitchen." He sent me a cheeky glance. "Marcus Hoare has a beautiful wife."

Something about his tone made my eyes widen. "Gerry. What are you saying?"

He chuckled. "Well, I'm not saying that I had an affair with the lovely Mrs. Hoare. But if I did, I might have billed Marcus Hoare for the hours I spent with her, too."

CHAPTER 3

*W*e were supposed to have a whole lunch hour to eat and recoup our nerves for the next round, but Gina had warned me the reality was snatching twenty minutes to scoff a sandwich and tea. The lunch buffet was pretty impressive, though: rows of freshly made sandwiches, an array of flaky pastries and muffins bursting with blueberries. We also got to try the other contestants' cakes, though the crew were quick to get their forks in too. I didn't have much of an appetite, but I knew I had to keep my strength up, so I loaded a paper plate and poured myself a reviving cup of hot, milky tea. I'd barely taken a bite when Gordon came up to me and asked to take off my mic.

"I was watching you in the first round," he said. "Pomegranate was a bold move, but you really pulled it off."

"Oh, thank you. I can't tell you how nervous I was."

"You shouldn't be. The camera loves you, that's for sure. I know everyone at home will be rooting for you. You're very likable."

I blushed. "It's hard not to feel like a wooden puppet

when you're talking to the judges and the camera's on you. It took all my strength to just keep stirring."

He pointed to my mic pack. "Remember that these are always on—some people are already giving away more about themselves than they should."

He gave me a knowing wink and strode off. Some of the contestants had already returned to their workstations to try and work out recipes or rearrange their ingredients. Others went off to have a cigarette break or just to sit and chat. I knew that I should try and mingle a bit and make some friends, but I had a plan of my own and tried to scuttle away without being seen.

I'd barely made my way toward the bridge that crossed the stream and led to the main grounds of the manor house when Gerry called my name. "Poppy? Hold on."

I liked Gerry, but right now, I wanted to slip away unseen. Him bellowing out my name was not helping. I gritted my teeth and tried to look pleasant as he came up to me.

"I thought you might want to practice your modest but delighted expression on me in case you win best baker today. Frankly, I think you've been far too modest. Your cake was brilliant. Traditional but with that lovely surprise twist."

"Oh," I said, flattered. 'That's very kind of you to say." I smiled and tried to think how I could still slip away. But Gerry was my strongest ally, and I liked him. "What are they going to do about your oven?" I asked.

He made a face. "Nothing. The electrician tested it, said it was fine and that it was my cake that was the problem. The cheek of it."

I tried to make him feel better by reminding him that we

still had two more challenges to show off our skills before the first episode was over.

He nodded. "One thing we can say for certain is that Evie's in trouble."

"Don't count your soufflé before it's risen," I said. "She could still outshine us this afternoon."

"I know. I know. But the poor woman was in tears. If that dear grandmother hadn't taken her in hand, I think she'd have done a runner."

"I agree. That's a tough blow to come back from. Still, I'm sure you've watched as many past episodes as I have, and you know it's never over until the judges make the final decisions."

I shuddered. Even just thinking about the public way that we amateur bakers were about to be judged made me feel sick to my stomach. At the end of every episode, one poor soul would be sent home. Honestly, I didn't even mind if it was me, but not on the first one. Not before I'd even had a peek at Broomewode Hall. I had bigger fish to fry than baking.

Knowing I needed to get away alone, I looked down and was almost blinded by Gerry's beautiful pure white sneakers. Bingo. "I'm going for a walk in those woods there," I said. "I need to get some air and clear my head. You're welcome to come with me?"

He looked dubiously toward the path leading into the woods. "What do you want to go in there for? It'll be full of dirt and mud."

"I know. But it will be private, and the cameras won't follow me."

He looked down at his clean white shoes. "Darling, in

these shoes, neither will I. Bought them specially for the show."

Phew. Exactly what I'd counted on. "Okay then. I'll see you later."

He grinned at me and turned back toward the tent. I felt a little guilty that I'd been less than truthful, but for what I had to do, Gerry would only be in the way.

Anxious to get going before anyone or anything else held me up, I strode purposefully toward the woods. The track was soft underfoot, and once I'd entered the wood, it felt shady and cool. The ground was covered with a bright carpet of bluebells, their dewy green scent filling my nose. I breathed deeply. I felt completely cut off from the bright lights and the madness of the filming crew. Before today, I'd no idea how many people it took to make a simple television show. I still didn't know what half of them did. They all seemed to be so busy and so stressed, running around doing jobs I really didn't understand. Here, it was quiet, and I realized that I hadn't lied. I did need to get away and take a minute. Once I was out of sight, I slowed my pace but not too much. I wanted to get a glimpse of Broomewode Hall. I guess if anyone was watching, it might look like I was a burglar casing the joint. But I didn't want to steal anything. All I wanted was to find someone, anyone, who might have information about my birth parents.

I set off in the direction of the big house so that I could quickly walk the perimeter of the manor and get a sense of the place. If I found the kitchen door, I thought I might knock on it another day when I had more time. My baking this afternoon would have to be spectacular so I'd make sure and have time to return. So no pressure then.

I was going so quickly, I actually burst out of the woods onto the manicured lawn with the most stunning view of Broomewode Hall. It really was a glorious manor house, its golden stone glowing in the morning light and the lead-paned windows reflecting the blue vista. As I was admiring the view, a man, or one who had been a man, strode around the corner. He stopped when he saw me. For a few seconds, we stood in silence, looking warily at each other. I was no expert on historical clothing, but he must have been an aristocrat. His outfit was elaborate, shiny black shoes with gold buckles, black breeches and a red cape lined with a thick layer of fur. His head was bare, but a sword hung at his side.

"And who are you?" he said, in a curt, imperious tone as though he were used to commanding people.

I felt a stirring of pity as I always did when I met spirits who seemed doomed to walk the earth. From his costume, I imagined he'd been alive several hundred years ago, and the sumptuous fabric of his attire probably meant that he'd been rich, important and probably titled. How difficult it must be now to have no substance at all.

Ghosts didn't usually realize that I could see them. Normally I made the first move. I said, in the soothing tone I used for spirits, "My name is Poppy. I won't harm you or try to chase you away."

He looked both taken aback and slightly amused at my words. "Well, Poppy, you're trespassing. I suggest you turn around and go back to wherever you came from. We are not open to visitors."

He spoke in a very modern way for a ghost. I narrowed my gaze and moved closer to get a better look at him. Normally if I concentrated I could see a shadowy line around the outside of the ghost, as though the difference in time zones or eras left a slight hazy rim around their edges. He said quite sharply now, "Are you listening? You can't be here. This is private property."

I wanted to get closer to show him I wasn't a threat, but I supposed that moving closer to a man armed with what looked like a very sharp sword was probably a stupid idea. "Who were you? In life?" I asked him.

Now an expression of alarm crossed his face. "Is there someone I should call? Someone who looks after you?" He spoke slowly as though I might have trouble understanding his words.

Before I could assure him that in my era it was perfectly all right for a woman to walk out alone without a servant following her, a female voice called, "Benedict?"

The man with the sword shook his head. "Surrounded by madwomen," he said softly to himself.

The voice came again, like a mother calling her recalcitrant child. "Benedict Arthur Champney. Do not make me call you again."

Somehow, I knew that this woman was very much alive, and I had no interest in being told by a real living person that I was trespassing, so I quickly slipped back into the woods until I was hidden from sight. By peering through the leaves of the tree I was hiding behind, I saw a woman wearing jeans and an expensive-looking cashmere sweater, her blond and silver hair in a sloppy up-do. The woman looked to be about sixty, attractive, and very regal. I recognized her immediately from the TV program. She was Evelyn Champney, Lady Frome. She walked right up to the ghost. "Benedict. You will be the death of me. Please, let's get this over with."

A horrible feeling crept over me. Was it possible that that man wasn't a ghost? But then why was he in those strange clothes? He must be. Which meant that Lady Frome shared my gift.

It was a mystery but one I couldn't solve now. We'd been told in no uncertain terms never to wander off onto the family's part of the property. It was strictly off-limits. I had no idea what the punishment would be if I was found trespassing, and frankly, I didn't want to find out.

I headed back down the path thinking that somehow I had to get past those two gatekeepers and find my way into Broomewode Hall. I'd been so tantalizingly close and been turned away by both the living and the dead. I'd gone through too much to give up now. I was determined to get inside the manor house and snoop. But how?

CHAPTER 4

*B*ack at the tent, everybody was too preoccupied with getting ready for the next round to notice I'd slipped away. I hurried over to my own worktable and frantically got my ingredients in order. My stomach was gurgling, and I realized that I'd barely eaten lunch, but there was no time for food now. We'd come to the final challenge of today's filming. Tomorrow, we'd get up and put on the same clothes (ugh) for the final showstopper challenge so it would look to the home viewer as though we'd done all three challenges in one day.

I wasn't nervous anymore because I was too tired to be nervous. This was going to be the make or break it round, and we all knew it. The cameramen were poised and ready. Gordon came over and re-mic'd me. "You had me worried that you wouldn't make it back in time," he said, as he made sure my pack was working and invisible.

"Sorry, I just needed some air."

"You're all right. Just don't cut it quite so close next time."

He gave me a thumbs-up. I smiled and took a deep breath as the judges and comedians swept into the tent.

Once cameras were rolling, Fiona gave Elspeth Peach her cue. "Bakers, you must be exhausted from your sponge-making this morning. But it's time now for your next challenge. It's a dessert I'm quite famous for, in fact." Even though I'd known this was coming, the now familiar wave of worry rippled through my body.

"We'd like you to make a tarte au citron. Every serious baker must master this classic, but it's certainly not as simple as it looks. We'll be judging your tarts by how well you balance the tangy lemon with its creamy counterpart and encase it in a rich butter pastry. Zingy and zesty is the name of the game. Best of luck to you all."

Arty and Jilly did a bit where Arty said, "You know what they say about life handing you lemons?"

Jilly put out her hands. "Make tarte au citron."

"Just what I was going to say." He smirked to the camera, and then he turned to us. "Bakers. On your marks, get set, bake!"

I swallowed hard and tried to smile in case one of the six cameras was on me. I'd watched plenty of episodes in preparation, and the first day was always the time when everything that could go wrong would. I didn't quite know the oven yet or the personality of the food processor. The whisks, knives and spatulas, all the bits and pieces that become part of your baking life, were all still a mystery. The only comfort I could take was that everyone else was in the same boat.

At least we'd had a chance to think about the tart challenge and practice. But it was tricky because the more carefully you combined your ingredients, the greater the risk of running out of time. I also still didn't know exactly how stiff my competition was. I knew Maggie was up there with the best. But who had it in them to thrive under pressure? Who was the dark horse of the show? All I could imagine was that this first week, everyone was out to impress the judges and win the hearts of those watching at home.

I began combining my flour and butter in a large glass bowl, then, using my fingers, gently rubbing the mixture until it resembled fine breadcrumbs. And then to my surprise, I saw Gerry slipping away to the toilet. I don't know how he thought he had time for the bathroom! I couldn't imagine even losing thirty seconds. Maybe nerves had gotten the better of him. But in fact, compared to the quiet terror all us contestants seem to be suffering with in the morning, this afternoon everyone was moving about the tent much more, talking to each other, even joking a bit with the comedian presenters. I guess we were getting into our groove.

I weighed out my sugar and added it to the mix, slowly introducing the eggs and water to make a dough. I was engrossed in rolling it out into pastry when I heard an enormous clatter. Marcus Hoare had walked past Gerry's station and knocked a mixing bowl over. "Whoops," he said, in a kind of fake horror tone that made me wonder if he'd done it on purpose. Gerry had weighed out his ingredients but hadn't yet mixed them, so Marcus frantically scooped the sugar back into the bowl.

The cameras caught the entire incident, but I doubted it'd end up broadcast. Florence caught my eye and then rolled hers in an exaggerated fashion. I laughed and turned back to my tart and began grating lemons. Their citric tang filled my nose and lifted my spirits. I followed the recipe I'd practiced so much I knew it by heart.

The rest of the meager ninety minutes went by in a blur. I went through the motions, trying to forget about the cameras, the strange sword-wielding ghost patrolling the grounds of Broomewode Hall, and my burning desire to get inside that building. I'd just finished decorating the pie with some candied lemon slices when I heard the dreaded clanger.

"Time's up, bakers," Jilly announced.

For the second time that day, I breathed a huge sigh of relief and plated up my tart, ready to take it to the judge's table. I'd tasted the filling, and if I said so myself, it was delicious.

"Now you all know that my dear Elspeth is famous for her delicious tarte au citron, so this is a tricky challenge, to say the least," Jonathon said. He regarded the table. "But it looks like we have a terrific array of tarts. I'm already salivating." He grinned. "This is going be a tough call, I know it."

I looked around, and all the contestants were smiling, trying not to look too hopeful. I was glad to see that Gerry was smiling too. I hoped he'd done well enough this time to discount the morning's earlier disaster. At this point, there was no telling what could happen.

One by one, the judges tasted the tarts. I don't know how they managed it—I'd be full to bursting after all that sponge, too. They praised three in a row before they got to mine.

"Now this, this is really something, Poppy," Elspeth said.

It took all of my willpower not to jump up and down on the spot with joy.

"I agree," said Jonathon. "An excellent marriage of zing and cream. Well done."

I was in such a thrilled daze that I almost missed what came next, but my ears pricked up when I heard a cry of distress. Elspeth's mouth was screwed up. "Oh dear, Gerry. I think you must have mistaken the salt for sugar. And your tarte looks so pretty, too. What a pity."

"How could that be?" he cried. "I measured out all the ingredients myself, and I brought a special sugar imported from France."

The production manager made a cutting motion to the camera trained on Gerry.

"I'm sorry, Gerry," Elspeth said softy. "Come here and try for yourself." She offered him a fresh fork.

Gerry crossed over to the judges' table and cut into his tart. When he swallowed, he grimaced. His face went ruddy. "I don't understand it. I just don't understand." He shook his head from side to side as if he were trying to shake water from his ear.

"Why don't you take five," the production manager gently suggested. "Get some air."

Gerry looked like he might argue but then turned and stalked out. If it hadn't been that judging wasn't over, I'd have followed. "Carry on filming," the production manager said to the cameras. The show had to go on.

Florence's tart won the round. She'd glazed the surface, generously dusted it with icing sugar and then, with a blow-torch, caramelized the sugar. She then decorated it in true French patisserie style, piping "citron" in melted dark chocolate. I was impressed! Florence bowed theatrically before the judges before curtseying at the camera. She was so good at being the center of attention. I envied her. I came third, after Florence and Evie. I couldn't believe I was in the top three.

"And that's a wrap for today," the production manager called out. "Well done, everyone. Bakers, clear your workstations and then get yourself to the pub!"

Filming had finally finished. The crew high-fived each other. I returned to my station.

I was shattered. Looking around me, the other bakers clearly felt the same way. Gina rushed over to me. She'd been behind the scenes all day, and I was relieved to finally see her.

"Poppy!" she exclaimed. "You were amazing. Dad's going to take all the credit, you know, for teaching you how to bake."

I pulled her close and gave her a bear hug, inhaling the familiar scent of her rose perfume, a welcome change from flour and lemon. "Boy, am I glad to see you. That was an intense day."

"I'm so proud of you, Pops. You're going to make it all the way. I feel it in my bones."

"Will you come have dinner at the inn? I've got loads to tell you."

"Oh, Pops, I wish I could, but I have to rush back now to babysit Reggie."

Reggie was Gina's nephew and the sweetest little boy alive. "Okay, I can't keep you from that little cherub, but tomorrow you're mine."

She kissed my cheeks. "Make sure you get plenty of rest tonight. Don't stay in the pub drinking with the other contestants. I've seen many a good baker on this show suffer with a sore head when they should have been at their best and brightest."

"Duly noted."

My heart sank a little as she dashed off. I really needed

my best friend to help me get through this. All the contestants were being put up in a local inn that was only a ten-minute walk down a country lane. It was owned by the Champney family that owned Broomewode Hall. My feet hurt, my brain hurt, and in about fourteen hours, we had to do this all over again. I didn't know how I'd manage.

After baking all day, I didn't even want food, but I knew I had to keep up my strength. My plan was to lie down for half an hour and then go down to the pub restaurant for dinner. Outside, the air was crisp, and the last of the day's sun shone on my face. I took a few deep breaths and tried to gather my thoughts before facing the rest of the contestants.

As the group walked the short distance, Gerry caught up to me. He was clutching a small plastic package. "Sabotage," he said, thrusting the package into my hands. It was the remains of a packet of sugar.

"What?"

"It's sabotage. Someone's out to get me. Here's the sugar I used. I didn't have salt anywhere near me when I measured out the sugar. And I'll tell you another thing. That oven is faulty. I don't care what that two-bit electrician said."

I doubted there was anything wrong with his oven, but I understood the impulse to blame the equipment. It was better than believing you were the worst baker on the show. "Oh, Gerry. It's just unlucky. We all make silly mistakes when we're under pressure. Tomorrow will be different, I know it."

He skipped over a muddy puddle on the path. "I'm serious. I'm going to get to the bottom of this. The electrician has invited some of the lads to play poker tonight at one of the cameramen's houses. I'm going to go and suss everyone out. Detective style. Want to join me? It's supposed to be all boys, but we could make an exception? Give me your best poker face."

"I'm incapable of one, and you already know it. I'll pass."

"You sure? I could do with someone on my side."

I caught a waft of expensive-smelling perfume and felt a warm arm slip around my shoulders. Florence. "Poppy's coming with us," she said to Gerry. "Aren't you, Poppy? She doesn't want to play silly boy games." She linked her arm in mine.

I laughed. "Why don't you join us," I said to Gerry.

He shook his head. "I've been in a temper. Focusing on cards will help. So will winning. Maybe see you for a nightcap—on me, if I win big, that is." He gave a sharklike grin. "I'm a very good poker player."

CHAPTER 5

The group seemed to split evenly into two when we got back to the hotel. Half went straight to the pub, and the other half went to their rooms. I followed Florence to the bar and thanked her as she insisted on getting the first round of gin and tonics and a packet of potato chips, or crisps as they called them over here.

We joined the others sitting on the soft red banquettes that lined the wall of the pub. Long-stemmed red candles flickered in empty wine bottles. The wooden tables were stained a deep mahogany. Hunting prints hung on the walls. Even though it was April and warm out, inside was as cozy as Christmas. The room smelled of roasted meat, and I looked forward to finally eating a proper plate of food. I was ravenous.

Florence clinked my glass. "Bottoms up, darling," she said, smiling. "Day one: done."

I took a long gulp. "Your sponge looked amazing this morning," I told Florence. "I never would have thought to do

Jack and the Beanstalk with tonka beans. So inventive. I was jealous."

She laughed. "Your myth scene was a masterpiece. I see the competition is going to be really tough." She gestured at the rest of the table. Three contestants I hadn't much of a chance to talk to yet were deep in conversation about the merits of polenta cakes. I remembered their names as Gaurav, Amara, and Daniel.

Florence lowered her voice to a whisper. "I feel simply terrible for Gerry. How unlucky to have his cake undercooked and then use salt instead of sugar. You'd think someone who renovated houses would have better control over appliances, wouldn't you?"

"I know what you mean," I agreed, taking another long sip of my drink. "He's convinced something was wrong with his oven."

"How very *male* of him," she drawled, making a sweep in the air with her polished red nails and rolling her eyes.

We got through the crisps so quickly, I went to the bar for another pack. The woman behind the bar looked at me intently for a moment, tilting her head and squinting slightly, before smiling at me. She had kind gray eyes and pale blond hair pulled into a long braid that lay over her left shoulder.

"Do I know you?" she asked.

"I don't think so. It's my first time here."

"And you're American. Never mind. One of the lucky bakers, I take it? Well done for making it through the first day."

"Thank you. I can hardly believe it."

She took the money from my hands and handed me the

packet. "Strange," she said, a quizzical look on her face. "You look so familiar. It's like I'm seeing a ghost I can't name."

I knew that feeling. Still, maybe I looked familiar for a different reason. A surge of hope raced through me. Could she know my birth mother? "Actually, I might once have had some family living around here. About twenty-five years ago? Maybe you'd know if they're still here?"

"Perhaps that's it. What were their names?"

Well, I hadn't thought that through very well, had I? I mumbled something about it being a cousin who'd married and I couldn't remember her last name. I must have sounded like a featherbrain.

She shook her head, obviously unable to recall who I reminded her of. This was the first lead I'd had since the behind-the-scenes documentary at Broomewode Hall, and so I said I thought my relative had been connected with the hall.

"If there's anyone around here who might remember, it's the cook at Broomewode Hall. She's been working there for over thirty years, and she makes it her business to know everyone else's, if you know what I mean. Katie Donegal's her name. I'm Eve, by the way."

She offered me her hand, and I shook it vigorously. "I'm Poppy. Thank you, thank you," I said. "That's so helpful. Do you think maybe I could visit her?"

"Don't see why not. She loves a natter and she adores the show. I'm sure she'd be happy to do a favor for a baker. If you like, I'll get a message to her and see if you can visit in the morning, before filming? If you can bear to get up that early!"

I was definitely not a morning person, but there was no way I'd let this opportunity escape me. "Absolutely. See if she'd mind just having a cup of tea or coffee?"

"Consider it done. I'll get a message to your room later, pet."

I beamed at Eve. Finally, I had a way into Broomewode Hall that didn't involve trying to creep past that strange guard. I was one step closer to finding out more about that blanket and hopefully where I came from.

I took the crisps back to Florence. Gordon, the sound tech, was sitting next to her, which was a surprise, as most of the guys had opted for pizza and poker.

"Not my scene," he said, shrugging.

Daniel, one of the other contestants, turned around. He had a head of thick, wavy silver hair but a youthful face and playful smile. "Me either. Sadly, my idea of a good night now is when all the kids actually go to bed at bedtime." He loosened the collar of his pale gray shirt.

There were murmurs of agreement at the table. "I love kids," Florence said. "Can't wait to have my own. How many do you have?"

"Three. Try having them at two-year intervals and then see if you feel the same way," he laughed, revealing a set of perfectly straight, pearly-white teeth.

"Let me guess—you're the dentist?"

"Guilty as charged," he said, holding up his hands in mock surrender. "But I have a wickedly sweet tooth. You wouldn't believe how many times a day I have to floss. I should get a sponsorship deal from one of the dental companies."

"Any time I hear the phrase 'guilty as charged,' I snap to attention and reach for my handcuffs out of instinct," Hamish piped up, laughing. He'd changed out of the blue and white striped shirt, which he'd worn during filming, and into a gray hoodie that matched his designer stubble. It made him look so much younger than I'd originally thought. He must only be in his mid-thirties. Hamish had also refused to join the poker game. "I find it boring," he said. "And I hate losing money. The way they were talking, I think the stakes will be high."

I hoped Gerry knew what he was getting into. In spite of his boasting, he could easily lose and I wasn't sure he could take another setback today.

I studied the menu, salivating over the classic British gastropub options: fish and chips, Lancashire hot pot, grilled gammon and chips. The waitress came over and took our order for dinner. Daniel began to order the steak and kidney pie but swiftly changed his mind. "Pie? What was I thinking? I couldn't look at another bit of pastry today."

The group chattered and laughed, and I was glad that everyone was friendly and not guarded and competitive like I'd feared. When the food arrived, you could have heard a pin drop, we were that hungry. I dug into my sausages and mash. They were swimming in rich red wine gravy, and I began to feel human again.

"So does filming cakes all day long give you the baking bug too, Gordon?" a contestant named Amara asked, tucking into a plate of fried hake covered in a creamy sauce. She was in her forties, and I'd overheard her discuss how happily married she was earlier. She spoke proudly about her two teenage twins, one boy and one girl, who were both in their first year of university, studying to be doctors like her.

"No. My wife used to bake." He came down hard on the K in bake, and there was a silence afterward, as no one knew what to say. Had she died? Left him? He didn't elaborate, and no one liked to ask.

"I'd love a new kitchen," Amara said, filling the awkward silence. "A bigger one, to be more precise. My husband is always moving things around, putting them back in the wrong place. I think the secret to a successful marriage is not two bathrooms, like people say. It's two kitchens!" She laughed and passed a bottle of red wine down the table.

I accepted a glass of wine and then tuned out of the chatter, scraping the remains of dinner from my plate. It was all I could do to hold myself back from licking the plate. But I got the sense that someone was watching me. Spinning in my seat, I turned around and saw a lady with an unkempt white, frizzy bob staring at me. She looked happy. Her eyes were wide and clear, and there was something very knowing in them. She took a step toward me, leaning heavily on a wooden walking cane, a duck's bill for its handrest. She was wearing a long navy dress made of linen, far too thin for this time of year, and a pair of orthopedic-looking shoes. I wondered if she was another ghost. I wasn't sure I could deal with a spirit right now on top of everything else.

"There you are, Valerie," she said, approaching my seat. "I've missed you. Where have you been?"

The whole table stopped eating and talking and looked at us. Well, at least that meant she wasn't a ghost.

"Valerie?" Florence asked quizzically.

"I'm sorry," I replied to the lady, baffled. "I think you've mistaken me for someone else."

Her eyes were cloudy but oddly compelling. "When are you coming to visit, dear? It's long overdue. I've missed you."

"Mum! There you are." Before I could answer, a woman

who looked to be in her forties rushed over to our table. She was red in the face but was clearly relieved. "You have to stop disappearing like this, Mum."

"Stop fussing, lovey. I'm perfectly fine. Look who it is."

She gestured at me, and her daughter looked baffled. I shrugged back, equally as clueless.

"I'm so sorry," she said, lowering her voice to address me. "Mum has dementia. She gets awfully confused. She used to work at Broomewode Hall, and she wanders back here all the time, like she's reporting for her duties again. I hope she didn't interrupt your dinner."

I shook my head no. Just as the woman was about to whisk her mother away, the old lady leaned forward and whispered, "Blessed be." She touched my arm briefly, and I felt the warmth of her touch through my shirt. I stared after the mother and daughter as they disappeared through the wide oak doorway. The strange part was that even though I'd never met the mother, I'd felt a strange sense of familiarity, too.

"Well, that was weird," Florence said.

Weird wasn't the half of it. Two women in the space of an hour had thought they recognized me. At least now I had a name, assuming the old woman had recalled the name correctly. I needed to find out who this Valerie woman was. Hopefully the cook at Broomewode Hall would remember her.

The waitress returned to clear our plates and asked if anyone wanted pudding. No one but Daniel could stomach something sweet after the day's baking.

"I wonder how the other boys are getting on at their poker night," Florence said.

"They're either brave or fools to play with Aaron Keel," Gordon replied. "That man has a terrific temper. I wouldn't play a friendly game of football with him, let alone bet."

I leapt up, excused myself from the group, and went back to the bar.

Eve was serving pints of Guinness to a group of men who behaved as though they'd already had enough. I tried to avoid tapping my fingers on the bar with impatience.

"Eve?"

"Yes, pet."

"Does the name Valerie mean anything to you?"

"Can't say it does. Why?"

"Not to worry. I'll put dinner on my room tab. I think I need an early night. This has been one long day."

I waved goodbye to the other contestants and retreated upstairs to my bedroom. It had the same oak floors as the pub below and a wide, inviting bed, plump with pillows and layers of soft cream blankets. Reading lamps emitted a warm glow from their ruffled shades. I slipped off my shoes and let my feet sink into the thick rug. My mind was whirring, but I knew I'd have to calm down before tomorrow's baking grand finale. My blouse wasn't too bad, though it was smudged with flour, and there was a slick of pomegranate on the collar. We weren't supposed to launder the clothes, though, as it had to look as though we'd done all three challenges in one day.

I hung up the less-than-pristine blouse, switched on the radio and decided to run myself a soothing bath. I folded today's jeans on a chair, slipped into the bathrobe kindly provided by the hotel and then put out fresh underwear for tomorrow.

Tipping the entire contents of a miniature rosemary and

bay bubble bath into the gushing water, I watched the foamy bubbles rise up from the marble tub and then slipped into the warm water. Heaven.

I leaned back and, with eyes half closed, watched the steam rise. I began to feel strange, as though I were floating, and then through the mist, I saw a playing card. The ace of spades. Before my bemused gaze, a drop of red slid from the bottom of the spade, like blood from a freshly cut finger.

I blinked and sloshed water as I sat up with a gasp. Usually when I daydreamed, it was about brownie recipes and the perfect way to toast almonds, not about cards and violence. I was tired. I needed to get to bed. I dried off and donned my pajamas, then padded out to the bedroom. I saw a note had been slipped under the door.

HI POPPY,

I got a message to Katie over at the big house. She'd be happy to meet you. Head over there at 8:30am and enter through the staff entrance at the northwest side of the house. She'll be there to greet you. Good luck with the baking, I'll be rooting for you!

Eve

I MOUTHED a silent thank-you to Eve. Tomorrow morning I might finally learn something about my beginnings.

CHAPTER 6

I woke from frenzied dreams when the alarm shrieked at six-thirty a.m. All night, I'd tossed and turned in the bed, hot beneath the heavy blankets, too cool when I threw them off. I couldn't get my mind to stop wondering about this mysterious Valerie, and I felt uncomfortable in my body, somehow. As I dragged myself out of bed, bleary-eyed and groggy, I was also full of a nervous excitement. Could Katie Donegal help solve these mysteries? And would I be able to keep up in the final baking challenge?

I showered and dressed quickly, anxious to start the day. I pulled a brush through my long hair and sighed. Gina could fix me up later and help me look a little more human.

Downstairs, the inn's restaurant was set for breakfast, but no one else was there yet. I wasn't going to make yesterday's mistake again, so I headed straight for the buffet. The food was beautifully arranged: silver trays of firm scrambled eggs, fried mushrooms, rashers of streaky bacon, and plump sausages laid out in a row like soldiers. Pots of thick Greek yogurt and ceramic bowls of fruit salad looked equally as tempting. I helped myself to generous portions and poured a large cup of black coffee.

"Easy, tiger," a voice said. "You'll split your jeans at that rate."

"Gerry!" I said, turning around. "I'd tell you how rude you are, but by the looks of you, you're already suffering." His green eyes were bloodshot, and his red hair was in even more disarray than usual. He also wore the same clothes as he had yesterday, but in his case, I guessed he'd slept in them.

"Ha ha. It's true. I might have overdone it slightly last night with a few too many whiskeys. But tell you what—it was worth it. I cleaned up at poker. Lady Luck was on my side, which is the least she could do after letting me down at baking."

We sat and Gerry, grinning, pulled out his wallet. It was dark green fabric and bulged with a thick wad of cash.

"Goodness, Gerry. You weren't exaggerating. There must be hundreds of pounds there."

"Enough to soften the blow of yesterday's baking disasters." He tucked into a piece of heavily buttered toast. "Told you I was good at poker."

We ate breakfast in peaceful silence, Gerry nursing his hangover and me trying to plot how I'd escape to Broomewode Hall without having to tell him where I was going. This was the second time he'd almost foiled my plans. Perhaps the bad luck had transferred on to me.

"What are you doing up so early, anyway?" I asked him.

"Ah, I can never sleep after a bellyful, and I was nervous about today, to tell the truth. Thought it'd be best to just get up and have the day done with. This way, I can get to my workstation early and watch them test my oven so I know it's done properly. After last night, I think I'll need to be careful around Aaron."

"Did you..." I didn't know what the proper term was.

"Cleaned him out," he confirmed. "Which was the least he deserved after not fixing my oven."

"Oh, Gerry, you're not still hung up about the oven, are you? I'm sure you just set the dial to the wrong temperature. It's easily done with new equipment."

"No, Poppy, something's up, and I'm going to get to the bottom of it."

I ate my last bite of eggs and stood. "I'm off for a quick walk around the grounds to settle my nerves."

"Don't be late!"

"I won't." As I set off, my watch read eight-fifteen a.m. Perfect timing.

It was another gorgeous spring morning. The birds were in the trees singing their sweet songs, the breeze was gentle, and I felt particularly blessed by an appearance from the sun, warming my sleepy face. I set off from the inn and strode purposefully up the cobbled path from the village toward Broomewode Hall. I tried to formulate all the questions bumbling around in my brain into something that wouldn't make me sound like a crazy person. I also hoped that it was too early in the morning to bump into the strange guard ghost/not ghost Benedict. So much was riding on the information from Katie Donegal. I couldn't afford any interruptions.

The old manor house was as impressive and imposing as ever, perhaps even more so being crowned by the rising sun. The flowerbeds were in full bloom, and the grass was still glistening with dew. I swallowed hard as I walked its perimeter in search of the staff entrance.

I eventually found the slightly less imposing door on the northwest side of the house. It had a huge brass knocker. I stood for a moment on the stone steps, hand raised in the air until I found the courage to rap the knocker.

I waited.

And then I waited some more.

I figured maybe no one had heard me. I rapped the knocker again, harder this time. Eventually, I heard the sound of quick footsteps vibrating along a stone floor. The door opened, and a woman of about my age was revealed. She was very petite, dark-eyed and dark-haired, and her lustrous locks had been twirled into an impressive bun at the nape of her neck. She wore an old-fashioned white crochet shirt, tucked into a black skirt and finished with a crisp white apron.

"Yes?" she asked in heavily-accented English. "How can I help?"

"I'm here to see Katie Donegal. She's expecting me."

"Mrs. Donegal isn't here this early in the morning. She doesn't start work until ten a.m. I do the breakfast prep. Are you here for the job?"

"No, no. I was supposed to meet Mrs. Donegal for tea this morning. She asked me to come at eight-thirty. I don't understand."

"Sorry. I'll say you came by." And with that, the door closed.

"But you haven't even got my name," I wailed through the wood. But I could hear the heels tapping stone, fading into the distance. I was truly and utterly perplexed. Mrs. Donegal was supposed to be my savior—not another mystery. I considered knocking again to see if anyone else would talk to me, but I didn't want to risk upsetting the staff or even getting myself evicted from the manor. There was nothing for it but to return to the inn and try somehow to get my head back into baking.

AT THE TENT, I searched for Gina, eager to tell her all about last night and this morning, not to mention needing her talents to work their magic on my tired-looking face. The other contestants were already there, setting up their work-stations and drinking mugs of steaming tea.

I found Gina, and with one look at my face, she sat me down in her hairdressing chair and said, "Spill."

I launched into everything that happened over the past twenty-four hours while she carefully painted my face and manipulated the waves of my hair into a style a little less scarecrow. She listened, interrupting only to tell me to stop moving my head. When I finished, she looked at me thoughtfully.

"That's so strange," she said. "I've met Mrs. Donegal a few times, and she's the most reliable, friendly woman around. She'd never agree to meet and then not show up. She'd be too excited to natter with a new person!" She paused and regarded my makeup. "Close your eyes again for a sec."

"I don't know, Gina. There's something very strange about Broomewode Hall. I just can't put my finger on what."

"All sorts of strange things happen here. They say we're sitting on top of an energy vortex."

I opened my eyes. "A what?"

She made me shut them again before saying, "It's like Glastonbury, only not as famous. They say there's a current of mystic energy that runs from Glastonbury, where King Arthur is said to be buried, to Broomewode Hall and beyond. You often see people in the village wearing beads and crystals and smelling of incense."

She put the finishing touches to my makeup, and I hopped off the seat. Marcus was waiting to have his face powdered. He looked as gray as Gerry had at breakfast. "Looks like someone's going to need a spot of fake tan," Gina said, giving him a professional once over.

"Take it you played poker, too, last night?" I asked.

He nodded. "I thought I'd learned how to drink hard and fast in the city, but that whiskey was lethal. I can't believe I've woken up with a stinking hangover *and* out of pocket to that thief."

"Thief?"

"Gerry robbed us all blind. Man's a cheat, I'm convinced. He was too clever to be caught, though."

"Come on now, Marcus. What was it you said yesterday? No one likes a sore loser?"

"I didn't lose. That's my point. I'm an excellent poker player. Making calculated wagers is basically what I do all day in banking. The only explanation is that I was cheated out of my money. Ask anyone who was there last night. Gerry did not win that cash fair and square. You should have seen the fuss Aaron made. Gerry took so much cash off of him— he's lucky he made it out in one piece."

Gina raised her eyebrows at me. Then said to Marcus, "Get in the chair. I can't make you feel any better, but at least you'll look good on camera." I wanted to stay and ask more, but time was pressing, and I needed to get my ingredients together for today's challenge.

When I got to my workstation, I found Jonathon Pine examining my ingredients. "Morning, Poppy," he said. "Just wanted to check in and see how you're doing. We don't get to speak to the contestants as much as we'd like during filming."

Now that I wasn't in the middle of baking, I could see that Jonathon had a kind, handsome face, not the severe features I'd expected of someone known for his tough critiques. His blue eyes were lively, mischievous almost, and despite his age, he still had a head of thick, black hair. He reminded me a bit of my dad, and I was struck by a wave of homesickness again. Jonathon was looking at me quizzically.

"I'm fine," I said quickly. "A bit overwhelmed, I think. But mostly I'm just really, really enjoying being here. It's an honor."

He gave me a wide, warm smile. "You're doing wonderfully. Do you find all the cameras unnerving? I do. I think I'm having a quiet private moment and look up to see two cameras trained on me."

I laughed. "I can't say it's not strange, but I think I'm already getting used to it. It is hard when the cameras zoom in to watch you put your cake into the oven, though. I always think at that moment I'll drop the lot onto the floor."

"Don't worry, there's only been a couple of droppers on the show's history. Everyone holds onto their tins for dear life." He smiled again. "I'll leave you to finish setting up." The cameras were heading my way to film me prepping. I tried to look amenable and open while also looking nonchalant. It was hard. Florence was at her station beside me, head down and frowning in concentration. "Good luck, Florence," I said.

"Good luck, dear Poppy," she replied in her languid way, raising her manicured hand to wave.

Marcus was the last one to arrive at the tent. As we all got our supplies ready, I saw Gerry call Aaron Keel over. The electrician's eyes were red-rimmed, and he did not look happy. He took two steps toward Gerry and said, loud enough for all of us to hear, "You complain about that oven again and I'll stuff your head in it." Then he stalked off.

"Told you he had a bad temper," Gordon said, fitting me with my mic pack. "I'm so glad I didn't join the game. I had a much nicer evening with two lovely ladies."

Was he flirting? He was so awkward it was hard to tell. Even as I looked up, startled, he was moving to Florence. He spoke softly to her, and she laughed. I shook my head at my own foolishness. He was just being friendly.

Soon Elspeth, Jilly, and Arty made their presence known. Elspeth came to the front of the tent and cleared her throat. Her white hair was twisted into an elegant chignon, and she was wearing a gorgeous peach trouser suit, perfectly tailored and glowing gold under the show's lights. I looked down at my comfortable jeans and re-tucked yesterday's shirt. I rubbed at a bit of lemon filling that had made a sticky mark on one sleeve. Despite Gina's herculean efforts with hair and makeup, I knew I was about to get covered in flour and food. It was about to begin all over again. I donned my apron. I took a deep breath. Blew it out.

"Bakers, your final challenge of the episode has been designed to test your skill but also your sense of innovation." Jilly paused and turned her smiling face to each contestant in turn. "Elspeth and Jonathon want you to bake a fruit pie with delicious golden pastry and excellent texture, but it must represent something about where you come from. This should be your showstopper."

She turned to Jonathon, who added, "We want to be wowed and astonished. I know you each have a masterpiece in you. Make sure your pie says something about your upbringing."

Jilly looked at Arty coyly and said, "I think my pie would say, 'should have paid more attention in school. There's no future in being the class clown.'"

"And look at you now," Arty said. Then, he turned to us. "All right bakers. On your marks, get set, bake."

This challenge had given me the greatest trouble when I'd been brainstorming ideas. Gina had suggested I create a pastry box with a pink marzipan baby inside. She was joking, or at least I hoped she was. In truth, it had taken some real soul-searching to come up with a good idea. The mystery of who I was had obsessed me for most of my life, but I really didn't want to share that mystery with a huge TV audience. This was a baking contest, not a therapy session.

Eventually, I thought about how much I loved being at the beach as a kid. I'd always been so happy when my parents told me we were going to the ocean for the day. I made endless castles in the sand, dug huge holes to bury my poor father in, and swam confidently in the ocean, silently goading myself to go farther, faster. I felt most free when I was in the water, weightless yet anchored somehow. I was never afraid.

So in preparation, I'd designed a seaside scene from the Pacific Northwest. I would do a granite rock with a few mussels clinging on, surrounded by a blue, glimmering ocean with some swirling seaweed detail. Of course, I couldn't make it taste like seafood (and wouldn't want to!), but I chose flavors that would be native to that part of America: hazelnuts and maple syrup and, naturally, being that I was from Seattle, coffee.

I was intrigued to see what everyone else was doing. This was such a personal task. Although baking always gave something of your personality away, this pie was going to be especially intimate. It forced us bakers to consider ourselves more closely. Amara was making a beautiful pear and cardamom pie, imbued with spices from her native India; Florence was making a toasted almond and cherry ricotta pie to represent her Italian roots. I couldn't tell what fruit Daniel was using, but he was fashioning giant fondant teeth that looked as terrifying as they did impressive! Hamish was making a pie inspired by the fluffy tail of one of his Shetland ponies. I overheard Gerry telling the judges that he was doing the four seasons because his job meant he was always outdoors. It was a great idea. He was using pear for fall, red cranberry for winter, strawberry for spring, then peach for summer. Maybe he was sucking up to Elspeth with that last choice of fruit, but I hoped he'd pull it off. He and Evie were both jumpy and even more nervous than the rest of us. It was clear that they were in trouble. However, any of the rest of us could screw up, and Evie and Gerry could pull off a masterpiece. It was still anyone's game.

There was no more time for eavesdropping or worrying about Gerry. I had to get my head down. I poured my energy into rolling hazelnut-flavored fondant into seaweed strips, curling the edges and spraying them with green food coloring. I was having trouble making them quickly. They were fiddly little suckers, and I was beginning to panic that I wouldn't finish. I was struggling with one of the strips when I felt Elspeth approach me. As much as I looked up to her, I was dreading having to talk at this tricky moment. I smelled her perfume, something figlike and green, before she spoke, so softly I wasn't certain I was hearing right. "Ah, a water witch. Of course. Poppy dear, just visualize the seaweed in your mind as you make them." And with that bizarre comment, she walked away again. Hmm, now if only what she said was true, that I could just imagine them into being and it would happen. But it was worth a shot, at least. I made sure that the cameras weren't on me, and then I closed my eyes for a few minutes. I pictured the Oregon coast, where we'd enjoyed so many family holidays, all the trips to the beach with my parents that I'd loved so much as a kid, and the swirling seaweed as the foaming ocean washed it up onto the sand. I felt my fingertips begin to twitch and move automatically. I suddenly sped up, spurred on and working double time compared with before. It was as if my hands had a life of their own. Goodness, I had no idea where this sudden—and much-needed—burst of energy was coming from, but I was extremely thankful that it had appeared.

By the time Arty warned us we had five minutes left, I was putting the final touches to my pie. I realized that I'd actually been having fun.

But that wasn't the case for everyone. I'd been so absorbed in my work that I hadn't noticed things had gone awry for Gerry again. He was hunched over his pie, shaking his head. I couldn't tell what was up. I hoped it wasn't serious and he was just being a perfectionist. Maybe that's what had been his trouble all along: He was just too obsessed with details and made foolish mistakes along the way.

But as Jonathon asked us to bring our pies over to the

judges' table, I saw that his pie was burned! The fruit was a charred mess. The should-be golden pastry was the color of mud, his fruit a charred, messy pulp.

I tried to catch Gerry's eye, but he was looking firmly at his feet. He wasn't the only one who seemed tense. We were a nervous dozen. Even Daniel, who was so chatty, tripped over his words as he was asked to present his pie and explain the decoration. The production manager asked us to reshoot that part, and Jilly told us a silly story about her dog to try and get us to relax. It didn't work. We were down to the final judging for this episode, and someone was going home. I felt sick to my stomach, as I was fairly sure I knew who that someone would be. I tried to keep a smile on my face for the cameras, but it wasn't easy.

Amara went next with her pear and cardamom pie. She'd grown up in Jodhpur and walked past the silk markets every day. She presented her showstopper, and Jonathon and Elspeth first commented on its artistic flair. She'd used spun sugar, icing and glazes colored with natural dyes from fruit to recreate bolts of brilliantly colored silks. Then each took a delicate forkful of the pie and judged its culinary merits. They praised the balance of the flavors and the richness of the pastry.

Evie was up next. They beamed as they ate her offering— a rum and coconut pie, inspired by her home country of Jamaica. She had clearly recovered from her disaster of the day before. I was glad for her, but it didn't bode well for Gerry. Then it was my turn. Jonathon was really taken with my coffee and hazelnut combination. "Perhaps even better than your sponge," he said to me, looking at his co-judge. Elspeth nodded in agreement. I glowed.

But Gerry was grim-faced as they called him forward. He was in trouble, and we all knew it. Jonathon and Elspeth both took the tiniest forkful of his burned pie. "It's burned," Jonathon said, stating the obvious. "The combination of flavors would have been lovely," Elspeth said. "What a pity."

The judging came to an end. Jilly got the honor of announcing episode one's best baker. "There's been some fantastic baking here today," she said. "Excellent flavors. Immense skill. Or at least that's what Elspeth just whispered to me. I couldn't tell a walnut whip from a wagon wheel myself."

There'd been several possibilities for the day's best baker, but none of us were surprised when Jilly called out Maggie's name. We all clapped, but I imagined each of us was dreading finding out who would be sent home.

That was Arty's job. His face softened, and I could tell he was going to be kind enough not to make any sort of joke. I was grateful.

"This is the hardest part of the show," he began. "I really hate having to do this. But it's my job to announce that the one baker leaving the show today will be..."

He paused and looked at us.

"Gerry."

Even though I wasn't surprised, I was still upset. Gerry was the only friend I'd made so far. He turned to me and gave me a brief smile. "Don't forget. Say nice things about me," he joked. But his eyes were sad.

I held out my arms and gave him a huge hug. And then, everyone seemed to be hugging everyone else. Marcus made a fuss of Maggie but didn't go near Gerry. He was noticeably smug. I hugged Maggie and congratulated her, and she said how pleased her grandchildren would be. Of course, this is where they would run the credits. It was hard to remember sometimes how we were part of a television show and that this scene had happened over and over for those who'd come before us and would happen again every week.

As everyone drifted back to their workstations, I went to console Gerry. I expected to find him upset, maybe even teary, but instead, he looked furious.

"I'm so sorry, Gerry," I said, putting an arm around him.

"Nothing to be sorry about," he said, "because I'm going to get to the bottom of this. I meant what I said yesterday: This is sabotage. Today was further proof." He raised his voice loud enough for the whole tent to hear. "I'm going to find out who sabotaged me this weekend." He stopped for breath, gathered himself and then said in a voice that reverberated around the tent, "And then I'm going to the press with my story—if it's the last thing I do."

CHAPTER 7

"*P*oppy," Florence called out in her silky voice. "Are you coming for a drink?"

The bakers had gathered outside and were murmuring about Gerry being childish and a sore loser. I had to admit that I'd been taken aback by his intensity. I couldn't believe he'd threatened to take his story public. I was worried about him, and I was worried about the show. But I was also concerned that he might have a point. He must have been an excellent baker to win a place on the show, and yet three separate incidents had occurred over two days and ruined all his hard work. Could foul play really have taken place beneath the safe space of our white tent?

He was still by his workstation, and Donald Friesen was with him. From the sounds of it, the series producer was irate.

"You can't go around making outlandish claims like that, Gerald," he said. "I know you're upset, but this is a serious allegation. You're risking the reputation of the entire show. We're an institution, greatly beloved by all of Great Britain and beyond. Be a good sport, and have your exit interview."

Gerry's face was nearly as red as his shirt. "The only thing I'll say on camera is the truth. Someone destroyed my chances, and they did it deliberately."

"You had some bad luck, but let's agree to put this episode, so to speak, behind us. Be sensible and do your exit interview properly."

"You've got more chance of the Queen of England joining the show to bake a jam roly-poly."

At that, Donald picked up Gerry's burnt fruit pie and threw it across the tent. It landed with a heavy thud on one of the potted ferns that lined the entrance.

Donald stomped off, muttering what I was sure were threats under his breath. A runner dashed to the poor fern and attempted to scoop the sticky remains of the pie from its leaves.

I whisked Gerry outside. Evening was approaching, and the air had cooled. I shivered and pulled my shirtsleeves tighter around me. "You didn't mean that, surely? About going to the press?" I asked him.

"Poppy. Something is really wrong here."

"Look, come for dinner at the pub and let's forget about the whole thing. You're off the show now, and there's nothing you can do about it, so why not enjoy a last supper with everyone and show them that you're a gracious loser?" I suggested, playfully digging him in the ribs.

"Couldn't face it. They'll be so smug. No, I'll pack up my recipe book and be on my way. Commiserate with a large scotch whiskey at home."

"But what about your things at the inn? We've all got to pack up for the weekend and head home till next week. Everyone will be doing the same thing."

"I'll get my bag tomorrow. I'm sure they'll keep it safe for one night."

"Don't be silly. Look. I'll pick up your bag for you. Then you won't have to come back."

"Poppy, I think I'm in love with you."

I laughed. I knew he was hurting, but at least he hadn't lost his cheeky sense of humor. Despite all the drama, I was going to miss him. He gave me his room key, and I told him I'd get his bag and meet him in the parking lot behind the catering truck. It was quiet back there, so no one would notice him waiting.

"Come to my workstation in the tent instead," he said. "There'll be no one left there. I want to take another look at that oven. Have a snoop around. I think I know who's behind this."

"Who?" I doubted it was more than bad luck but was still curious.

But he only shook his head. "Wait until I'm sure. Then I'll tell you."

I saw Florence walking back up the road. She'd wrapped herself in a luxurious-looking black cashmere sweater. Her knee-length skirt was silky and caught the light. I waved. She skipped the rest of the way and tried to pull me back to the pub to have drinks. Everyone was waiting for me so that they could crack open a bottle of fizz to celebrate Maggie's win and our joint safety for another week. She tugged at my arm and pouted at Gerry and told him not to be a party pooper.

"Go," Gerry said. "Have yourself a glass of bubbly and then meet me back at the tent in half an hour?"

"I demand an hour, Gerry," Florence said.

He agreed, and Florence and I raced back to the inn.

Apart from Marcus, everyone was there, and the fizz was flowing. I accepted a glass and clinked to Maggie's success, all of our successes really, but I had one eye trained on the bar to see if Eve was working. I wanted to get to the bottom of what happened this morning with Katie Donegal. But it looked like Eve was off tonight. It would have to wait until next week. Maybe that wasn't such a bad thing; I'd certainly had my fill of drama for one weekend. What I really wanted was peace and quiet, a hearty meal before packing, and then head home to my own bed for the week. Bliss. I already regretted telling Gerry I'd pick up his bag. But he'd been so nice to me, and I felt so bad for him that I wanted to help in whatever small way I could.

We sat down, and everyone began praising Florence's show-stopping pie. Maggie thought that Florence should have won today's best baker. She asked her about the beautiful pastry decoration that crowned her ricotta pie.

"It's *sfogliatella*. Like a lobster tail. They're a classic shell-shaped Italian pastry. It's so hard to make each section look like little leaves. I was worried I hadn't sliced it thinly enough."

"It was perfect," I said, "just like your cakes yesterday."

She smiled and then asked me not to leave before we all had dinner. I reminded her that I'd promised to drop Gerry's bag because he was too embarrassed to come back to the inn.

"Don't want to be late for your boyfriend," she joked.

"Not funny," I said. "I'll only be ten minutes."

"Just don't be a soft touch, okay? I have my suspicions about Gerry. I don't think he's as nice as you think he is."

I wasn't worried. I didn't imagine Gerry and I would stay

in touch, but if I could do him a favor after he'd been the one sent home, maybe someone would do the same favor for me when my time came.

Upstairs, no one noticed that I slipped into Gerry's room instead of my own. His black duffel bag was on the desk, already neatly packed. I checked the bathroom, but he'd packed everything, even his toothbrush. It was as though he'd suspected he might be the first one out and wanted a speedy exit. I was sorry he'd felt that dejected, but also pleased I didn't have to pack his stuff.

I hoisted his bag over my shoulder and then slid out again. I cast a longing glance at the staircase back to the pub, but I wanted to give Gerry his bag so he could get on his way. Dinner could wait. Poor guy had had a real weekend of it. At least he'd won a stack of cash at poker, though. He could take some solace in that. No one saw me go downstairs through the lobby, and soon I was walking down the now familiar lane back toward Broomewode Hall.

There was a security guard sitting in a lawn chair when I got close to the tent. I explained my errand, and he nodded and let me pass. It was getting dark now, and without the bustle of cast and crew, the white tent looked ghostly. A cool breeze ruffled my hair and sent a chill through me. I kicked myself for not getting a cardigan back at the inn. I'd give Gerry his bag and get back to the nice, warm inn and enjoy a hearty dinner in the pub with Florence. And then I'd make a renewed effort to meet some more of the other contestants. I didn't want to face the rest of the show without friendly faces around me. It was hard enough without feeling alone, too.

I took a step forward but then jumped a mile when a black shape moved in the evening's fading light.

The shape resolved itself into a black cat walking daintily toward me. I breathed out a sigh of relief. "Well, hello there," I said, dropping down to cat level. It came closer but not quite in petting distance. It stopped and stared at me through gorgeous green-gold eyes. I waited, and in a few seconds, she came closer and rubbed against me like she'd known me all her life. She had a glossy coat and a friendly manner. I searched for a collar or tag but found nothing. "You look too lovely to be a stray. Who do you belong to?" I'd always loved cats, and I felt less alone now that I had a feline friend. "I bet you keep the mice in that old manor house on their toes," I said. The cat looked at me as though I weren't the sharpest knife in the drawer. Still, she didn't walk away, and her coat was so silky, I kept stroking her. She gave a soft, sweet purr.

The duffel was heavy on my shoulder, so I got up again, waved the cat goodbye and headed into the tent.

I noticed a strange odor, like something was singed. Perhaps it was remnants of Gerry's charred pie. "Gerry?" I called. Nothing. It wasn't dark yet but dusky enough that he could be standing between the fridge and his workstation and I wouldn't see him. He hadn't put a light on, but I knew which station was his. It was odd walking through the tent without the hubbub of the show. No mixers whirring. No peals of laughter from Arty and Jilly as they cracked up at their own jokes. Only an eerie silence.

I thought I heard something moving. Poor Gerry, no doubt he was saying a final goodbye to his workstation, maybe giving his apron a farewell hug. As I got closer, a strange feeling made its way down the back of my spine, as though something was after me. I turned, but there was nothing there, only the cat. She must have followed me. "Hello again," I whispered. "You gave me a fright." She circled my ankles, and I bent down again to give her a stroke. "You'll protect me from bumps in the dark, won't you, sweet thing," I whispered. She meowed back.

The darkened tent was spooking me out. I had a strong impulse to turn and run, but I was just strung out and overwhelmed by the last few days, it was making me jumpy. There had been so much anticipation and buildup to this weekend, it was no surprise I was experiencing the fallout. I called Gerry's name again, louder this time. He didn't answer, but I felt there was someone in the tent with me. That I was not alone. "Who's there?" I called out quite sharply.

There was no reply.

I was definitely creeped out. Since Gerry had specifically asked me to meet him here and I was already doing him a favor, I didn't feel inclined to hang around. Something must have held him up, maybe another altercation with the series producer, and dinner wasn't going to wait forever. I decided I'd leave his bag at his station and write a quick goodbye note. I was about to put the bag onto his countertop when I saw a dark shape on the ground. I bent over and looked closer.

It was a man lying face down and very still. He was wearing very white running shoes. "Gerry?" My voice wavered. Had he fallen? Fainted?

I was about to touch him when I felt as though unseen hands were pulling me back. I got out my mobile phone and put on the torch and then gasped and scrambled backward.

Gerry had his hands outstretched as though reaching for his oven. There were black burn marks on his hands. Science wasn't my strongest subject at school, but I could put together that a guy on the ground beside an electrical appliance, with burn marks on his hands, could've been electrocuted. Touching him was probably a very bad idea.

I had to get help and fast. I scrambled to my feet and ran back to the security guard. He took one look at me and got to his feet. "Miss, what's wrong?"

I pointed a shaking hand toward the tent. "In there. A man's hurt. Electrocuted, I think. Call an ambulance."

His eyes narrowed on me for a minute as though I might be joking. When it was obvious I wasn't, he grabbed his walkie-talkie and began speaking into it even as he jogged toward the tent.

I fell to my knees, out of breath and in shock. "I think he's dead," I whispered into the dark. As if she'd understood me, the cat appeared out of nowhere and leapt into my lap. She tucked herself into the crook of my arm, and I stroked her soft fur. I stayed crouched like that, trying to process what had just happened. Less than an hour ago, Gerry was ranting and raging, and now he was motionless on the floor.

With every fiber of my being, I hoped he had just passed out. That it was a small shock. Nothing more serious than that. I raised my head and looked back to the tent, half-hoping I'd see Gerry stumble out of the entrance with an embarrassed grin on his face mumbling, "I'm fine, I'm fine." But an instinct told me that was never going to happen.

When the security guard came out of the tent alone, his expression told me what I most feared was true. "Never had no one die on my watch before," he mumbled, wiping his mouth with the back of his hand. And then I heard the wail of sirens coming from a distance.

I wouldn't believe it until a doctor had confirmed my suspicions. But, like the security guard, I was pretty sure Gerry was dead.

CHAPTER 8

*I*n the few minutes before the ambulance arrived, the sky turned a purple shade of black. The cat stayed by my side, and she looked on kindly as the tears dropped from my eyes. I studied the blades of grass and ran my hands across their soft tips. The security guard shuffled from foot to foot, mumbling, "Never seen a dead body before," to himself over and over again, which really creeped me out. Time felt stretched out before me, endless and surreal. It was like I was in a bubble or swimming under water, closed off to anything that wasn't in my direct eye line. It wasn't until I heard a man's voice saying, "Miss, Miss, are you okay?" that I looked up.

It was a solemn-looking police officer. He wore plain clothes, but his short hair and very demeanor told me he was a cop. From my position on the ground, he was extremely tall. He extended an arm and helped me to my feet. "I'm Sergeant Adam Lane."

I stared at him for a moment. He had a long Roman nose, deep-set warm brown eyes, a full mouth and a clean-shaven face. His flop of dark brown hair was much longer than I'd expect from a police officer, and he was, indeed, extremely tall. I was taken aback. "Poppy Wilkinson," I said, brushing the grass from my jeans and smoothing down my shirt. "I'm a bit..." I trailed off, not sure what I was. Shocked, grieving, frightened, disbelieving. My emotions were such a mess, I couldn't isolate a single one. "I found him."

"Miss Wilkinson, do you feel up to answering a few questions?" he asked gently, as though I might have a choice in the matter. Naturally, the police wanted to interview me.

"Of course," I replied. He walked me back toward the tent. In those endless minutes I'd been crouched on the grass, a host of people had arrived. The grounds were awash with paramedics, and members of the crew had turned up, including the electrician, Aaron Keel, and Donald Friesen, who was striding around the now sealed-off tent, looking like he was pulling his hair out. When the police set up lights, it was almost as if we were about to shoot another episode. I couldn't decide if it was more or less spooky than when it was dark.

We walked over to the entrance of the tent, where another man was standing, talking to a paramedic. "Miss Wilkinson," Sergeant Lane said, "this is Detective Inspector Reid Hembly. He'll be leading the investigation."

He looked to be about twenty years Sergeant Lane's senior, with a gray buzz cut and a square jaw. His white shirt and navy trousers were crisp, and everything about his appearance was exacting, shined shoes and gleaming fingernails that must have been scrubbed until they felt raw. "You must be very shocked," he said. "But could you talk me through what happened here this evening?" DI Hembly spoke to me the way my father did when I was struggling to understand something. I found his manner soothing.

"How did you come to be in the tent? What did you notice? No detail is unimportant."

I nodded. I tried to focus on the officers' faces and not on the forensic team, and someone I could only assume was a pathologist or maybe the coroner now surrounding Gerry's body. I told them who Gerry was and everything that had happened this evening—Gerry's continued problems with the oven, how he was voted off, his suspicions of sabotage, and ending with how he decided to come back and check the oven.

I'd volunteered to bring him his bag and how I wished now that I hadn't. If he'd been at the pub picking up his duffel, he wouldn't have been in the tent. He might still be alive. I tried to include as much detail as possible. When I'd finished, I took a deep breath. "Was he...was the oven faulty?" I looked around. "I mean, he had burns on his hands. He was electrocuted, wasn't he?"

"It certainly looks that way," DI Hembly said. "But we need to make some thorough checks before we jump to any conclusions." He looked around at the tent all set up with its dozen kitchens. "Was it a very competitive group?"

"No. Not really."

"Did Gerry have any enemies?"

How could I answer this without buying into Gerry's wild accusations? "He told me he thought he knew who'd sabotaged his chances, but when I asked him who it was, he wouldn't tell me." I shook my head. "I think he might have said that to sound dramatic. I can't imagine anyone would want to hurt him seriously. It must have been a faulty oven, as he said."

"There was nothing wrong with that oven," Aaron Keel said in a tight, angry voice. I started. I hadn't noticed him standing nearby, but there he was, peering at the electrical panel. A police constable stood watching him.

DI Hembly frowned at him. "Thank you, sir. We'll be with you in due course." Then he walked me farther away, out of earshot of the show's electrician. No wonder Aaron Keel was snarly. An electrocuted contestant wouldn't do his career much good, and we'd all heard Gerry complain that his oven was on the fritz.

We settled at the long table where we'd eaten lunch earlier in the day.

"Apart from you, did anyone else know that Gerry would be here at this time?"

Oh, good question. I looked at the detective and tried to recall. As though he really were my dad, I wanted to give him the right answer. "Florence overheard us making the plan. In fact, I said I'd meet Gerry in thirty minutes, and she told him to give us an hour."

"Florence?" The sergeant had his notebook open and was writing down what I said. It was as disconcerting as having a cameraman follow me around when I was baking.

"Florence Cinelli. She's another contestant. Her tarte au citron won one of the challenges." And that was so relevant to the investigation. *Way to go, Poppy.*

Donald Friesen came charging toward us. He was red in the face, and beads of sweat were gathered at his temples.

"Tell me this is all a nightmare and I'm about to wake up," he said to no one in particular. He put his head in his hands. "My career's just gone up in smoke." Then, obviously realizing that wasn't the most sensitive phrase, he said, "Sorry, Poppy. My brain is fried. No! That's not what I meant." He looked at the two detectives. "I'm the series producer. Let me know how I can help."

"Are all the cast and crew still here?" DI Hembly asked him.

"They're having dinner together, and then they'll start leaving."

"Please make sure no one leaves until we've spoken to them. We'll interview everyone this evening."

"But it was bad wiring. That's got nothing to do—"

"We'll need to talk to everyone tonight."

Donald looked as though he might argue, then made a sound like the air letting out of bread dough when it's punched down. He headed off in the direction of the inn, shaking his head from side to side.

A photographer had arrived to take photos of the scene, and a small crowd of investigators were gathered around Gerry's body. It was all very surreal, like watching a cop show on TV, except I seemed to be one of the actors. And I did not know my lines or how the plot turned out.

"Sir?" someone called. "I think you should see this."

"You head back to the inn now, too," Sergeant Lane said. "We'll come down and find you shortly."

I remembered poor Gerry's duffel bag and told the sergeant he'd find it on the floor near Gerry, where I'd dropped it.

He gave me an encouraging smile and his dimples flashed, then the two detectives pulled on latex gloves, slipped protective covers over their shoes, and headed toward the action.

I started back down the lane toward the inn when I saw Elspeth Peach walking hurriedly toward me. She was still wearing her peach suit but now with the addition of a scarf wound around her neck. "Poppy," she said, a little out of breath. "Thank goodness you're okay. I sensed that you were in danger."

A wave of emotions hit me, and the full force of the evening's events was finally unleashed. "Not me," I said, welling up. "Gerry. Oh, Elspeth, Gerry is dead!"

"Dear child, what on earth are you talking about? He was sulking his way out of the tent just a short while ago."

Through my tears, I managed to tell her everything. My voice was shaking, and when I finished, she leaned in to hug me. "My poor child."

I felt something circling my ankles and nearly screamed, but it was only the friendly black cat. I bent down to pick her up. "Hello again," I said into her fur. "You're quite the persistent kitty."

"Ah, I see you've chosen each other," Elspeth said. I held the cat closer to my chest, and she nuzzled into the crook of my arm.

"I think she's lonely. Maybe a stray."

"Don't worry, Poppy. Things are already working themselves out," Elspeth whispered. I looked at her quizzically. "You can trust the cat. She'll protect you from harm. Come on now, let's make our way back to the inn. I'm sure you're famished, and I fear we've a long night ahead of us. Take this cardigan to keep warm." She pulled a thick sweater from her bag.

"How did you know I was cold?"

"Instinct, dear."

She offered me a tissue, and I took it gratefully, dabbing at my wet cheeks, embarrassed that I'd cried in front of the great Elspeth Peach. Although funnily enough, she no longer felt like a stranger or like a celebrity that I'd looked up to all my life. No, I felt strangely close to her now. She felt more like family, a beloved great aunt, perhaps, even though we hadn't spent more than five minutes alone together.

We ambled down the lane in friendly silence. I couldn't manage a conversation. My mind was whirring with everything that had happened. On top of the stressful baking show, I'd found Gerry dead. It was all too much.

When we got to the inn, I reluctantly put the cat on the ground before going inside. All the contestants were gathered in the pub talking and exclaiming loudly as Donald tried to hold their attention.

"Poppy!" Florence called out. "There you are! I was worried sick. Where have you been? Donald says there's police all over the grounds and we can't leave."

Everyone turned to face me. No doubt my face was a mess, streaked with mascara and tears. They all stared, as if they expected me to explain everything.

I opened my mouth to speak when Elspeth flashed me a kindly look and said, "Bakers, I'm afraid there's been a terrible, terrible accident." There was something so calm and soothing about Elspeth. After Donald had wound everyone up, she seemed to bring the stress level down in a few sentences.

Yes, the police had asked everyone to wait so they could speak to us all, but she was sure it was only routine. Everyone should go back to eating their dinner or whatever they'd been doing. The police would be with us as quickly as they could.

It wasn't long before Sergeant Lane came in. With him was Jonathon wearing a leather jacket, with a weekender bag slung over his shoulder. "I was about to drive away," he said, "when I got the word." He looked around, his blue eyes coming to rest on me. "Everyone else all right? Poppy, horrible for you. Can I get you anything?"

I shook my head, grateful that he cared.

"What's all this about us not being able to leave?" Marcus asked, sounding annoyed. "I've an important job in the city."

Sergeant Lane said, "We'll need to speak to all of you, I'm afraid."

"But I don't understand. It's very sad that Gerry died, but people die every day." He gestured to all of us. "We only baked with him. We didn't know the man. It's nothing to do with us."

"In the case of such an...unusual death, I'm afraid we have to be very thorough in our investigation, sir."

Amara went forward, and in a soft voice, I heard her ask when they might be allowed to leave. I needed some quiet, so I slipped away to my room.

I WAS PERCHED on the edge of the bed when a knock on my door broke my reverie. I stood, surprised at the interruption of my whirring thoughts.

"Poppy? It's Florence. Open up."

I opened the door. Florence had changed into black silk

trousers and a loose-fitting blouse. She held out a bag of sweet popcorn and a wrapped sandwich. "How are you holding up?" she asked. "Elspeth asked me to bring you a sandwich. But the popcorn was my idea. Sweet snacks? To take our minds off things?"

I smiled at her weakly, and she flung her arms around me. I was soothed by the soft, powdery scent of her perfume. I was glad she was there. I'd tried calling Gina, but her phone was off. She'd left right after filming ended, on babysitting duty again. I wondered whether the police would want to interview her anyway. I'd had a missed call from my parents, no doubt desperate to hear about the day's events. I'd thought about returning the call, knowing how well they could console me, but I didn't want to worry them by telling the truth. It would have to wait until more was uncovered about Gerry's death.

"You must be feeling absolutely wretched," Florence said.

It was a strange phenomenon, losing someone we hardly knew. But some of us had also bonded with him quickly. Although it had only been a weekend, the intensity of the show meant I felt like I'd already known him for years.

Florence swept her long hair into a neat bun at the nape of her neck and then opened the popcorn. "How are you holding up? I don't think I could handle seeing a dead body." She shuddered delicately.

I paused for a moment. I saw them all the time, just in ghost form. "I'm fine. I mean, I'm sad. Kinda spooked." I shook my head as she offered me the packet. I was struggling to get through the egg and watercress sandwich, though I knew Elspeth was right. I needed to eat. "But I'm confused, too. I still don't understand what's happened. The police are acting like it's a suspicious death, but Gerry kept saying it was faulty."

"He also claimed he was being sabotaged. There might have been foul play," she said, settling on the bed and pulling her knees up to her chest.

"But why? Who would hurt Gerry? He was already off the show."

"Who knows? Gerry managed to make enemies in a short time," she said, frowning.

"What did the police ask you?" I got up from the bed, pulled the heavy red curtains shut and switched on another lamp. It cast a warm glow across the room.

"It was Sergeant Lane. He's a dish, isn't he? Well, he asked about my movements for the whole day. I mean, crazy detailed like how long I took for lunch, everyone I spoke to today, if any strangers had been loitering on the grounds. It took ages. He wrote every little thing I said down in his notebook. It made me feel like *I'd* done something wrong."

I gulped. I didn't want to tell the police I'd spent the morning knocking at the staff door of Broomewode Hall. How could I possibly explain what I'd been doing there? But withholding information from the police wasn't an option. I was going to have to tell the whole truth and hope it didn't make *me* sound suspicious.

"You know," Florence said, leaning forward as if she were telling me a secret, "being holed up in here is making me feel strangely guilty. Like *we're* the criminals."

Her voice had a touch of drama in it, and it dawned on me that in a weird way, she might be enjoying the day's events, the drama of it. I dismissed the thought, though, as cruel. Surely only a psychopath could revel in someone's death.

"*And,*" she continued, "I'm also a bit worried about my own safety. I mean, is there a lunatic wandering the grounds of Broomewode Hall?"

Yes, I thought. *His name is Benedict, and he plays dress-up and wields a sword.* "Goodness," I replied. "I hadn't even considered that."

"It makes you wonder who you can trust here. Just to think, this morning everything was fun and games. I mean, we're literally on a game show. But now..."

She trailed off, and her deep brown eyes bore into mine, full of sadness. I didn't know what to say. Nothing was making sense. Florence kept eating the popcorn, though I was surprised to find that she could eat at a time like this. As if she read my mind, Florence said, "I eat when I'm stressed. It's a curse for my waistline. Sure you don't want some?"

I shook my head. There was a loud knock at the door.

"Miss Wilkinson? It's Sergeant Lane."

"Just a sec," I called back.

"Oh gosh," Florence whispered. "I'm in for it now! He'll wonder what we're plotting."

"Don't worry," I whispered. "Say you were feeling scared. I have a feeling you'll play a very convincing damsel in distress."

I opened the door. "Sergeant Lane," I said.

"Miss Wilkinson...and Miss Cinelli, too, I see."

Florence said, "I knocked on Poppy's door to make sure she was holding up okay and to bring her some food. I was just leaving." She scooted past Sergeant Lane and gave me a brief wave on her way out.

"You've had a traumatic day. I'm glad you have someone

looking out for you." He smiled. Those dimples. "We need to ask you some more questions downstairs."

I took a deep breath, gathered my thoughts and followed him down to the private room they were using as an interview room. He shut the door behind me with a bang that made us both jump.

CHAPTER 9

The inn had a private dining room, which had been made into a makeshift interview room. A quiet contestant named Gaurav, whom I'd barely seen all weekend, was just leaving. He was tall and slim with a permanent bashful look on his face. When I'd first heard him speak, it was in a soft Birmingham accent. He was demure and liked to use ginger and cinnamon in his baking, two of my favorite ingredients. His cakes looked delicious. He flashed a small smile my way. I returned it and made a mental note to talk to him more; he seemed nice and maybe a little bit lonely on the show. But then I caught myself. After what Florence had said about not knowing who to trust, I was already second-guessing my instincts. I'd just have to keep my barriers up until all this nasty business was over.

Detective Inspector Hembly was seated bolt upright in a wooden chair placed at the head of a long, antique-looking dining table. In a row on the wall behind him hung three oil paintings, each depicting a fruit: a bowl of cherries, a ripe-looking pear, and a bunch of glossy purple grapes. Through a square, latticed window I could see the light of the moon throwing a pearly gauze over the sprawling fields of Broome-wode Hall. Three low-hanging chandeliers lit the room, making an oddly romantic atmosphere for a situation so serious. Deadly serious. In front of DI Hembly was a small paper notepad and two black pens. He looked up as I came in and Gaurav left.

"Miss Wilkinson. Please take a seat." He pointed at the chair opposite him. Sergeant Lane sat beside him, notebook open and ready.

I crossed my legs at the ankles and gathered my hands in my lap so as to avoid fidgeting. It was like being interviewed for college or my first job. I was more nervous than I'd been filming all weekend, more worried than when I was staring into the depths of the oven, praying for the sponge to rise. Florence was right: I felt tremendously on edge, as if I'd committed a crime. I told myself to calm down and try to stop sweating.

Detective Inspector Hembly talked me through the interview procedure, telling me they just needed a clearer picture of the day's events. He gave me his usual, fatherly expression. "I understand from the others that you were closest to Gerry."

A pang of grief hit me sharply. "Yes. I didn't know him well, obviously. We only met yesterday, but we'd sort of teamed up. We promised to help each other get through this."

"Did you notice anyone unfamiliar loitering around the set or on the grounds of Broomewode Hall?" he asked in a brusque but not unfriendly voice.

The sudden change of subject jarred me, as perhaps he'd meant it to. "No, nothing at all. But to be honest, there are so many people involved with filming the show that I'm not sure

I'd notice who was meant to be there and who wasn't. The crew is huge, and I haven't spoken to all of them. It's hard to keep track."

He nodded, his eyes on me, but I didn't know whether he was trying to be kind or examining me for signs of lying. I tried to arrange my face into something resembling neutrality, like I'd seen Florence do, but I think the effect looked more like I needed the bathroom.

"Did Gerald get along with everyone in the cast and crew?" DI Hembly continued. "You mentioned earlier that he felt he was being 'sabotaged'?"

"Yes. But I'm sure everyone heard him say that."

"Could he have been telling the truth?"

"His baking was a bit of a disaster. First his cake was undercooked, then his lemon tart was salty, and finally, his pie was burned. That was why he went back to the tent to check the oven. He was so certain something was wrong with it. I never should have let him go back there alone."

"You weren't to know," Sergeant Lane said gently.

I paused to think and order my words. "He managed to make some enemies this weekend, but it was small stuff. Nothing anyone would kill over."

"You'd be surprised," DI Hembly said in the tone of one who'd seen it all.

I stared for a moment at the painting of the pear above his head. How alone and vulnerable it seemed, marooned on the vast canvas with its rippling layers of brown and gold oil paint.

"I suppose first it was Marcus."

"Marcus Hoare?" Sergeant Lane confirmed, scribbling in his notebook.

"Yes. The banker. Actually, there's something you really need to know." I felt awful tattling on Marcus like we were in school, but for Gerry's sake I had to tell the police what he'd told me. "They knew each other before the show."

The two detectives exchanged a glance. I had no idea what it meant. Had Marcus told them about Gerry and his wife? Or not? Maybe they hadn't even interviewed him yet. "How did they know each other?" Detective Inspector Hembly asked.

This was hard. How could I explain it tactfully?

"Gerry and Marcus knew each other because Gerry did some work on Marcus Hoare's house. Gerry said he'd known Marcus's wife...quite well."

"Are you saying they had an affair?" Clearly, the detectives weren't interested in tact.

"He didn't say that in so many words, but it was the impression he gave, yes."

DI Hembly tapped his fingertips on the scarred dining table. "I see."

"Gerry is...was...quite playful in nature. But Marcus acted like they'd never met—even when they were face-to-face.

"And yesterday, Marcus knocked over one of Gerry's bowls during filming." I gasped. Why hadn't I seen it before? I leaned forward. "It was the challenge where Gerry's tarte came out salty instead of sweet. I was so busy with my own tart that I didn't pay much attention at the time, but I saw Marcus spill Gerry's sugar and swiftly put it back into the bowl. Now I wonder if he did replace some of the sugar with salt?" And I'd pooh-poohed Gerry's assertion that his tart had been tampered with.

The sergeant wrote notes, but neither of them seemed overly impressed with the salt-instead-of-sugar story.

"Anything else?"

I explained what happened when Gerry was voted off the show and how irate Donald Friesen had been when Gerry threated to go to the press, throwing his burnt pie across the tent. The whole exchange had only taken two minutes, but it had shaken everyone up a bit. Donald was supposed to be in control, the senior and reliable member of the production crew. For him to have acted out like that was deeply unsettling. Once more, they both seemed underwhelmed by my news. No doubt everyone who'd been there had already told them about the Friesen incident.

"He also had words with the electrician about the oven. Told him he didn't know the first thing about appliances."

I stopped, embarrassed on Gerry's behalf. He'd been so kind to me, it was difficult to believe that he'd managed to upset three people over the course of the weekend. But now, saying all of this out loud, I realized that Gerry had certainly not been a saint.

"Anything else you can think of?"

Before I could answer, there was a knock at the door and a young paramedic stuck her head around the door. She was red-cheeked and panting, as if she'd been running. "Sorry to interrupt, sir," she said, "but I think you might want to see this." Sergeant Lane stepped out of the room. DI Hembly looked at me expectantly.

"No," I answered. "We didn't talk about anything serious. I didn't really know anything about his life except that he renovated houses and was considered to be pretty good at it." I stopped, suddenly remembering our conversation over breakfast. I'd been so worried about having to explain why I went to the manor house in the early hours that I'd completely forgotten about last night's poker game. "Detective Inspector Hembly, I don't know how it could have flown out of my brain like this, but I also saw Gerry this morning at breakfast. We were both up early. Gerry was pretty worse for wear with a hangover. He'd played poker with some of the contestants and crew last night. It was a bit of a boys' night. I'm not sure who was there, but Gerry won the game. He really cleaned up. Marcus was convinced Gerry had cheated."

He nodded. Again, this wasn't news. No doubt someone who'd been present would give them a list of who'd played and how much they'd lost.

The door opened, and Sergeant Lane returned holding something in a sealed plastic bag. He set it down on the table.

"Gerry's wallet!" I exclaimed.

Sergeant Lane looked at his boss and raised an eyebrow. "How did you know that?" he asked.

"I was just explaining how Gerry played poker last night. He showed me his wallet this morning, and it was stuffed full of cash. A big bundle of notes. He was bragging about his win. I don't think some of the guys were so happy about his winning streak." The wallet was the kind hikers use, made of dark green fabric and held together with Velcro. Easy to recognize, except it was a lot slimmer now.

"You're sure the cash was in this wallet this morning?" Sergeant Lane asked me.

"Yes. He showed me the money and then put it back."

"There's nothing in it now but Gerry's gym membership and driver's license."

The two officers left the room. I heard them talking in

hushed tones outside the door, but I couldn't make out any words. My head was all over the place. How could someone rob a dead man? Or was he mugged beforehand? Was there really a person out there so mad at Gerry that they could kill him? I shook my head. This was a bad line of thinking, and I refused to go down that road. I stood and began pacing the room. A large wood and glass cabinet housed three shelves of crystal glassware. A brown leather chesterfield couch fit snugly between two pillars. A black Inglenook fireplace took center stage at the back of the room, a neat pile of logs flanking each side. So many happy occasions must have taken place here. Birthday parties, anniversaries, maybe even a small wedding reception. And now it was being used for a police enquiry.

I leaned against the window and rested my head against the cool glass, looking out into the dark grounds of Broome-wode Hall. The gardens around the inn had been planted with beautiful whitebeam trees, and in the faint moonlight, I could just make out their bushy green leaves swaying in the breeze. How could somewhere so tranquil and lovely become the scene for something so terrible? I was staring into the dark when a sudden sound startled me. Was that a meow? I looked up, and sure enough, the black cat was prowling outside the window. She looked cold and stared at me, clearly asking to be let in. "Hi, sweet thing. I thought you'd scampered off," I murmured, pushing up the window.

The cat wasted no time stepping inside and jumping to the ground. She circled my ankles, rubbing her little pink nose into the folds of my jeans. I bent and lifted her into my arms. Her fur was chilly, but I thought I received as much comfort as I gave. "How did you know I was in here? Was

Elspeth right? Are you my little guardian angel now?" She mewed in response. "Well, I'll have to give you a name. Can't just be calling you cat now, can I? You need a suitably sweet one. Crumble? Strudel? Waffle?" The cat looked at me, unimpressed. "No? You don't like those? How about Gateau?" She began to purr. "Gateau it is, then. At least until I find your real owner." Gateau was French for cake, and she was absolutely as sweet as any cake I'd ever eaten. I could see her in my cottage, sitting in a chair, watching me bake. I hoped Mildred would take to her all right.

The door opened again. "Miss Wilkinson?" It was Sergeant Lane.

"Honestly, please call me Poppy. I've never been called Miss Wilkinson in my life."

"You're holding a cat."

Nice bit of detective work.

"Yes. She followed me this evening, and I heard her mewing outside, so I let her in." He seemed to like cats, so I told him I'd named the cat Gateau.

His dimples deepened when he laughed. Florence was right; he was a dish. "I'm a hero with my niece since I turned up with two strays. Brothers. Fortunately, my sister let her keep them. She named them Slush and Squidgy."

DI Hembly came back into the room. He stared at me and shook his closely shorn head, seemingly baffled.

"She followed me," I said by way of explanation. He obviously decided to ignore the crazy cat lady and continue with more serious police business. I guessed he came across eccentric people all the time in his line of work. I was all ready to tell them about my unauthorized visit to Broomewode Hall and, if pressed, I'd even tell them why I wanted to know more about the place. However, instead of asking for my movements all day, he merely said, "Thank you for your help. You'll need to stay tonight, but the production company will cover the cost."

I wasn't surprised, but if they were keeping all the contestants overnight, they must suspect something bad had happened to Gerry. I thought of his empty wallet and felt like I'd been kicked in the stomach.

As I left the room, I saw Marcus Hoare lurking at the end of the corridor. He was white in the face and clenching his hands together. I didn't know where to look. I hadn't liked the guy, sure, but I still felt bad that I'd passed on gossip about his wife. I walked by him without speaking, just a small nod, Gateau still curled against my shoulder. She made me feel calmer. I hoped the inn owners wouldn't chastise me for bringing an animal inside and decided to take her straight to my room.

I climbed the stairs, weary and even more perplexed than I'd been before I met with the police. At least my room was cozy. I locked the door behind me and flopped onto the bed. The small digital radio on the bedside table read ten p.m. It felt more like three a.m. Gateau hopped onto the bed and made herself comfy on the blanket. I lay down alongside her, tucking a plump white pillow beneath my head, and listened to her soft purrs. I was caught somewhere between exhaustion and being so agitated, I couldn't even imagine sleeping. The empty wallet mystified me. I thought back to the morning. It seemed like eons ago. Gerry had certainly shown me a wad of cash, but there couldn't have been more than a couple of hundred pounds in notes. Not enough to kill for, surely?

Gateau raised her head and looked at me inquiringly. Her

little paws plowed the bed covers. "What is it?" I asked. "Are you trying to tell me something?" She raised herself up and trotted back to the bedroom door, scratching at the wood. "Aha. Are you hungry, little one?" She mewed. "I'll try and find you some food. And I should eat, too." That sandwich earlier hadn't been very substantial, and now my stomach was gurgling. There was nothing for it but to go back downstairs and see if I could scavenge anything from the restaurant.

I'd only made it halfway down the stairs when I heard the commotion. Aaron, the electrician, and Donald were in the hallway, yelling at each other. I couldn't get food without going past them. It was super awkward to head into a wave of angry syllables. "I will not be responsible," Donald said.

"Nobody's asking you to."

"If this gets out—"

I stopped in my tracks as Aaron turned and saw me, a look of pure fury stamped on his face.

Just then, Inspector Hembly opened the door and walked out with Marcus Hoare. He was even more pale than before he'd gone in.

"Sergeant," DI Hembly said in a somber voice, "can you please gather everyone in the interview room? There are a few things I'd like to explain to the group before some of them can go home."

Donald looked at me, and I knew I shared the same concern on my own face. The phrase *some of them can go home* had struck fear into both our hearts.

CHAPTER 10

The crew and contestants assembled in the main pub dining room. Fortunately, there didn't seem to be any other guests, and no doubt locals had been told the pub was closed for the evening. It was strange to see everyone together outside of the tent and so late in the evening, too. The strains of the day were showing: blue circles under the eyes, tired grayish skin, and worried brows. As I looked at everyone in turn, I was struck by how familiar they were to me now. Maggie seemed to be looking after Evie and Florence. Daniel and Amara were deep in conversation. Two contestants I'd yet to really chat with, Euan and Priscilla, were sitting by the fireplace, which had now been lit. Gaurav was standing alone, tapping away at his phone.

I thought about my phone upstairs and wished hard that I could phone my mom and dad. Nothing could sound so nice as my parents' voices right now telling me everything would be all right. I also missed my cottage, the way the ivy crept over the windowsills, the old stone walls, so full of history. I even missed Mildred, my dear kitchen ghost. Elspeth caught my eye across the room and gave me a reassuring smile as Jonathon talked urgently into her ear.

The room was warm, the fire adding cheer to the depressing atmosphere, but voices were hushed. Everyone was waiting to be told what was going to happen. The anticipation was tangible.

Sergeant Lane and DI Hembly entered the room. Everyone fell quiet and stopped what they were doing. Euan and Priscilla stood up. It was like a school assembly and the headmaster had walked in. I couldn't shake the feeling of being in trouble.

DI Hembly cleared his throat. "Thank you for your cooperation while we conduct our investigation. I realize many of you wish to return home this evening."

There were murmurs of agreement from the group.

"Unfortunately, I'm only able to let some of you go."

A low groan and a ripple of chatter erupted through the group.

"But I need to get back to my kids."

"Work will fire me if I'm not there in the morning."

"I've just found out my dog is sick."

Detective Inspector Hembly interrupted. "Our priority here is ascertaining exactly what happened to Gerald Parterre."

"If he wants me to stay, he'll have to arrest me," I heard Marcus mumble behind me but not loud enough for the police to hear.

"Who's going home?" Amara asked.

"We ask you all to keep your phones on in case we need to ask you any questions. Sergeant Lane is going to read out the names of those we need to stay this evening. The production company has kindly agreed to pay for any of you who wish to stay for another night. However, if your name is not on the list, you're free to leave."

The room fell silent again. It was like waiting to see who'd been voted off the show, except this time, we were all secretly praying to leave. Sergeant Lane brought out his little black notebook. "If the following people could please remain behind: Florence Cinelli, Poppy Wilkinson, Marcus Hoare, Aaron Keel, Donald Friesen, Gordon Bennett and Hamish MacDonald. The rest of you are free to go."

My heart sank, but I wasn't surprised at hearing my name. I'd been the one to find the body, and I'd given information about Gerry's arguments. I could have argued that I didn't live very far away and could drive back first thing. Still, I was so stressed, I shouldn't drive. I resigned myself to another night at the inn. Maggie and Evie both opted to stay. They were tired and upset and had too long a journey to face it now.

Gordon Bennett walked over to me and gave me a hug. "I haven't had a chance to say how sorry I am. That must have been awful," he said. "Finding your friend that way. I hate that you had to see...that."

And suddenly I saw Gerry's body on the ground. The silly cars and trucks all over his red shirt, the bright white trainers. He'd been like a little boy in some ways, as though everything was a game, from playing with clients' wives to poker. Someone, though, had been deadly serious.

"Thank you. Poor Gerry. He was so young. So full of life." I was puzzled that his name had been on the list and said so.

He made a face. "They want my technical expertise. I'm on standby to help them go through all the hours of recordings."

I'd never thought before about how tedious most police work must be. And how dull Gordon's job must be a lot of the time. "Do you mind very much?"

He considered my words. "Not really. It's rather interesting to be in the thick of a police investigation."

"Are you a fan of thrillers?"

Before Gordon could reply, Donald strode to the front and addressed the group, just as we were about to disperse. "Guys, can I have your attention for just one more minute? I'm not sure what's in store for the show this week, but rest assured we're going to do our best to get everything sorted and continue filming next week. In the meantime, for those of you who are staying, the kitchen staff is putting together some food for us. I'm also arranging for the rushes from today's filming to be shown on a small projector in here, so at least you'll have something fun to watch. It's a real treat seeing yourself on screen for the first time."

He attempted a small laugh, but no one joined in. Despite his polished speech, Donald looked very tense indeed. The hairs at his temples were stuck to the skin with sweat. Veins bulged along his neck; his eyes were bloodshot and full of fear. In short, he looked...guilty. I supposed throwing that burnt fruit pie across the tent felt like a pretty stupid move right about now. But he also had my sympathy. The entire production rested on his shoulders, and who could imagine a worse disaster than a suspicious death?

Florence rushed over to me as soon as he finished talking. "I don't understand it," she said, shaking out her mane of glossy hair. "Why could they possibly want me to stay? I don't know anything."

"Don't worry," I said. "I'm sure they're just covering their bases. Maybe you told them something of interest in your interview that they want to follow up. I'm sure it doesn't mean anything bad."

"I don't like this one bit. And I'm hungry...*again!* This stress is going to wreak havoc with my figure. Where's that buffet?"

As if on cue, a couple of tired-looking staff came into the room with trays of food. They pulled a trestle table resting against one wall upright and laid down their dishes. Ham sandwiches, egg sandwiches, and slices of cold roast chicken were set down, and a plate of fruit, cheese and crackers joined them. There was tea and coffee or anything we wanted to order from the bar. It all looked extremely tempting. The room began to empty out as the contestants who wanted to leave made their excuses. Florence asked if I wanted to stay and watch the rushes, and because I knew I wouldn't be able to sleep after all this tension (not to mention the coffee I couldn't resist), I agreed. We pulled up two chairs and munched our way through the food as a couple of the crew who were left set up a projector. From the corner of my eye, I watched Elspeth and Jonathon continue their whispered talk. Elspeth looked serious and firm, Jonathon determined—like he was trying to persuade her about something. I was intrigued.

As the food reached my empty belly, I started to feel better. I was savoring a particularly succulent slice of roast chicken when I remembered that poor Gateau must have scampered off to forage for herself. I excused myself to Florence, revisited the chicken platter, and placed a few choice cuts inside a paper napkin.

Cold air hit me as I followed the corridor in the direction

I'd seen Gateau go earlier. The rest of the inn was deserted and lit only by a few lamps, which were mounted to the wall-papered walls in pairs. Their burgundy shades threw out a soft glow.

"Gateau? Where have you disappeared to? I've got treats."

The sound of voices caught my attention. Two bodies were pressed up against the door to the inn's back entrance. I stopped in my tracks. "Goodness," I whispered to myself. It was Jilly and Arty, and they were locked in a passionate embrace! Did they even know they were allowed to go home? Did they want to?

I turned on my heels and tiptoed off in the opposite direction. What an odd pairing, but I was glad something nice had come out of the weekend. Still chuckling to myself, I continued my search for Gateau.

I couldn't say why, but I had the feeling that she was by the kitchen door. In fact, I *knew* it. A strange sensation was sweeping through my body, something like a pulling motion, almost magnetic. The skin on the back of my neck got goose-bumps. It was just like the moment I discovered Gerry's body, when I was about to touch him, but something compelled me to draw away. No, pulled me back. I picked up the pace. My legs carried themselves faster and faster, operating like they were under the influence of some other being. It was then that I recognized Jonathon's tall silhouette by the kitchen door. In his arms was Gateau. I was about to greet them when it dawned on me that Jonathon was talking to the cat. And what's more, she seemed to be listening. I cocked my head and tried to understand what I was seeing. Because from here, it looked like those two were having a fully fledged gossip.

Jonathon turned toward me, and for a brief second, pure shock crossed his face, but in a flash, he'd composed himself again and grinned. "Look what I've found." He presented Gateau like a gift, as if he were returning her to me. "Elspeth told me you'd adopted a stray."

"She's been following me around this evening. I couldn't find a collar or owner, so I'm going to look after her until I do. I'm not sure if she is a stray, but I've named her Gateau."

The cat squirmed out of Jonathon's arms and circled my feet.

"I see you've chosen each other," Jonathon said.

"That's so weird. That's exactly what Elspeth said."

Jonathon smiled. "Maybe Elspeth and I have been spending too much time together lately. Clearly we're rubbing off on one another."

I bent down, unwrapped my chicken parcel, and offered her the treats. She sniffed at them, seemingly bemused, and then carefully began to eat. "She's so refined," I said. "I feel like she's asking me for a dish to eat from."

"Perhaps she is," Jonathon mused. "Come, let's go back and see what the day's rushes look like."

I followed Jonathon, Gateau happily trotting behind us, and asked why he and Elspeth hadn't left with the others. "I suppose we both feel a bit protective. This is my first season, of course, so I don't want to ditch and run at the first sign of trouble. We'll see how things look tomorrow. We're not supposed to get too friendly with the contestants, obviously, until the judging is all over, but this is not a normal situation." He said they'd stay the night and longer, if necessary, and make themselves available for anyone who wanted to talk. "Pastoral care," he said. "Plus, Elspeth has a secret supply of clotted cream fudge from Devon in her room, and she's willing to share."

Back inside the dining room, the smell of freshly brewed coffee engulfed me. I was already sure I wouldn't sleep tonight, so I poured myself another cup. Those left were eating heartily and sipping from big ceramic mugs. Jonathon more sensibly chose Earl Grey, and Florence made space for us at the table. She was watching the screen avidly. "Isn't it so exciting to see what we all look like?" she asked, though it was more of a statement. Since she was a drama student, I suspected she already knew what she looked like on film. I had a strong feeling she'd look better than any of us.

The cameras were trained on Florence as she stirred cream into her lemon mix. And, yep, she looked wonderful. Her skin was glowing, the whites of her eyes and the whites of her teeth gleaming as she laughed that throaty laugh of hers. Her silk blouse caught the light as she moved. "You're a true Hollywood beauty, Florence," I said. "Born for lights, camera, action."

She glowed even more in response. "Gosh, what's that?" she asked, looking down at Gateau.

"She's followed me about this evening. Isn't she the most gorgeous thing? I'm adopting her until her owner surfaces."

Florence bent down to stroke the cat, but Gateau shied away from her touch.

"Aww, why doesn't she want to play?" Florence asked in a babyish voice.

I didn't have an answer for Florence. To me and Jonathon, Gateau had been extremely affectionate. I shrugged off her question and let Gateau nestle in by my feet.

It was odd how the atmosphere in the room had changed.

The tension had eased away. Those left behind at the inn were eating and chatting like it was a slumber party. Only Donald Friesen exuded anxiety and paced about the room as he watched the rushes. He appeared to be checking his own pulse intermittently and picking the skin around his fingers. Poor guy. Aaron hadn't stayed. I had no idea where he was.

Hamish, the baking policeman, headed over to us. He smiled at Florence and then laid a friendly hand on my shoulder. "How you doing, Poppy? You've had quite the day." There was something comforting about Hamish, like a big brother. His hair was up at odd angles from running his hands through it too often, and his brow was rippled with lines, but his shirt was a trendy plaid. Maybe it was something to do with being a police officer; there was a firmness about him, but he seemed compassionate and caring too. Over the course of the evening, he'd been reassuring the whole group, keeping everyone calm and explaining the stages of an early investigation. It was normal procedure, he'd said, and no one should be distressed.

Having a cop on "our team" was comforting. I could talk to him in a way I couldn't to the police investigating the case. I asked him the question that was beginning to obsess me. "Do you think Gerry was murdered?"

I hoped he'd laugh at such a foolish suggestion. Explain that the police were only doing their due diligence before proclaiming a tragic accident. He didn't.

"Seems likely," he said, not in a dramatic way like Florence, but as though he'd looked at the evidence and made a rational conclusion.

"But why? Who?" I asked.

His green eyes warmed when he smiled. "That's what the

police will have to work out. I'm happy to say I'm here to bake, not solve a crime."

"Why did they ask you to stay?"

I thought he'd shrug off my question, but after glancing around to make sure no one was listening, he dropped his voice. "In truth, they didn't. I volunteered. I don't like leaving knowing the killer is still out there and likely involved in this production."

Well, I had asked. Now I felt both reassured that he was staying to guard us and frightened because he felt he needed to. Florence gave a little squeal of distress, "How can they make us stay in a hotel with a murderer?"

"If they believed there was any danger, they wouldn't have you stay. But I know there will be police officers on duty all night." He hesitated then said, "And I'm in room three if you need me."

Luckily, Florence was back on screen so her attention was diverted back to the rushes.

The three of us settled in to watch. When I came on the screen, I cringed. There wasn't any sound yet, and this made it all the more bizarre. Everything about my face was so *large*. My cheeks were too pink, and I recognized my panicked look, my eyes darting from bowl to mixer. Jilly had obviously just cracked a joke, and I broke into the fake smile I'd practiced.

I was amazed at how much footage there was and began to admire the editing team who'd have to pull all the pieces together to make one episode.

There was Maggie, putting on her glasses to check the recipe. Gaurav, gesturing as he explained something to Jonathon. Marcus Hoare walking the short distance to the ovens to check on his sponge.

There was Evie dumping her first batter in the bin. That was painful, but worst of all was watching Gerry, so cheeky and full of banter, as he joked with Arty and Jilly. And there he was again, taking his sponge out of the oven. First in proud anticipation and then increasing horror as he realized it hadn't baked properly.

If he was going to die, I so wished he'd had a good first episode so at least his final hours would have been happier.

The rushes continued, but I felt weird and twitchy. Something was bothering me, like a name on the tip of my tongue, an elusive memory. But what was it?

Since six cameras caught bakers at different times, everything was out of sequence. Here I was taking my tart out of the oven. At least it wasn't obvious how tight I was gripping that tin. I turned to ask Hamish and Florence if they were as terrified of dropping the goods as I was, but they were deep in conversation about the proper way to make a panettone.

I turned back in time to see Marcus take his tart out of the oven. And then I felt like someone had stuck a pin in me, that's how sharp the shock was. "Wait," I said aloud. "That's a different oven."

I looked around the room to see who else had spotted it. Donald was yelling into his phone. Elspeth was talking quietly to Jonathon. Hamish and Florence were still nattering on about the Italian Christmas bread, and everyone else must have gone to bed except Marcus Hoare. He was staring directly at me. I'd never seen a person look more afraid. Or more caught out.

"What were you doing at Gerry's oven earlier, Marcus?" My tone must have been tense enough that the two beside me stopped to stare.

"Nothing," Marcus said. "You're overtired, Poppy. You should go to bed."

Oh, yeah, patronizing me in that snooty way was a really good idea right now. Even Donald had ended his call and was listening. "Didn't anyone else see it? Earlier in the rushes, Marcus is checking his sponge in an oven, only it's not his oven. It's Gerry's."

With everyone staring at him and knowing all we had to do was rerun the tapes to prove I was right, Marcus did his best to look unconcerned. He shrugged awkwardly, nearly strangling himself on his buttoned collar. "So I checked on the competition. That's no crime. I probably peered in your oven, too."

Beside me, Hamish said, "No. But if you also sabotaged another contestant, one who was later murdered, that is a very serious crime." I was so glad Hamish was sitting here beside me, solid and tough. "Donald, let's play those rushes again. Poppy, tell the police what you've told us. They should see this footage, too." He turned to me and said, "Well done, Poppy." I felt like an honorary copper.

"This is ridiculous. I'm not sitting around here to be insulted," Marcus said, getting to his feet and moving toward the door.

I stood too. I was not going to let Marcus leave. Behind me, I heard mumbling coming from Elspeth. I couldn't catch the words, but I felt as though a streak of power went past and through me. Marcus went to open the door, but it wouldn't budge. He tried again, throwing his weight against it. The old oak door could have been in its original tree form for all the budging it did.

Suddenly, it opened from the other side, and Marcus fell into Sergeant Lane's arms.

"Hold that man," Hamish said, and Lane obliged, looking at us all curiously. Rapidly, Hamish related what I'd seen.

Marcus stopped struggling and stepped back, trying to sound cool. He didn't succeed very well. His voice was high and jumpy. "I didn't kill anyone. I've got nothing to hide."

It didn't take long for Donald to replay the relevant footage. "See?" I said, there's Marcus checking an oven, but that's not his oven. It's Gerry's." As I watched the sequence for the second time, I caught what I'd missed earlier. "And, look, he's changing the temperature."

"You're certain that's not his oven?" the inspector spoke to me, but Donald answered. He sounded livid. "No. Poppy's correct. That's Gerry's oven. So he was right all along. He was being sabotaged."

"Right," DI Hembly said, walking toward Marcus. "We'll continue this down at the station." He placed a firm hand on his back and walked him out of the room. At the door, Marcus paused and turned. The loathing in his eyes turned my blood cold. I'd made an enemy—and even worse, it was a potential murderer.

CHAPTER 11

The following morning, I awoke to find Gateau gone. I'd left the window ajar, and she hadn't stayed the night. I felt a pang of sadness, but I was sure that she'd be back soon. It had taken me a long time to fall asleep. I'd tossed and turned, tangled in the inn's soft sheets, but nothing was comfortable. I was haunted by Marcus's chilling look, the way hatred had emanated from his entire being.

I roused my groggy body and considered the events of the previous evening. When the police had taken Marcus to the station, the relaxed mood of the dining room soured. No one knew what to say and quickly returned to their rooms. That someone involved in the show might be responsible for Gerry's death was a terrible shock for us all. And despite Marcus being down at the station, the atmosphere was one of quiet fear. Florence and I hugged and promised each other that we'd have each other's backs since our rooms were directly across the hallway from each other. However, nothing had disturbed me all night but Gateau making herself comfortable on my bed and my own dark thoughts.

I pulled the thick red curtain aside and let the morning light filter into the room. It had rained overnight, and the breeze carried the scent of dewy grass. From here, I could just glimpse Broomewode Hall, its golden stone glinting in the early sun. A carpet of crocuses were in bloom, vividly purple. The grounds of Broomewode Hall were refreshed and unchanged. It was unsettling, as if yesterday's terrible tragedy had never happened. How I wished that were true. I knew that even if the police let us, I couldn't go home today. There were now two mysteries that I would not let go unsolved: Gerry's death and the identity of the enigmatic Valerie.

Since I was sure the police had the best suspect in custody, I could focus on my personal detective project. I'd go back to the manor house—and this time, I wouldn't be fobbed off at the staff entrance. I'd go straight to the front door. If yesterday had taught me anything, it was that life was precious and things could change in an instant. I had no time to waste. I was going to have to become my bravest self and find a way into that building, come hell or high water.

I dressed in the only skirt I'd brought with me. It was black, and with it I wore a blue-green camisole and a cream-colored linen shirt that was a favorite, which I wore open like a jacket. I put a bit more effort than usual into my hair and makeup and was just slipping on my shoes when there was a knock at the door.

No. Not now, Florence, I said to myself. I'd have to tell her to go away. But as I grew closer to the door, I knew it wasn't Florence. I felt calm and glad as I opened it.

Elspeth was standing outside. "May I come in?" she whispered.

Surprised at the secrecy, I nodded and stepped back. She

shut the door behind her. "Jonathon and I aren't supposed to get too friendly with the contestants, but we won't talk about the competition. That's not why I'm here."

"All right." I wondered why she was standing in my room at eight o'clock in the morning. She was dressed much more casually than usual, in jeans and a T-shirt, with a long cardigan overtop. She'd left her hair long. She looked like someone's very cool grandma. I wished she were mine.

She smiled her kindly smile at me and said, "I've brought you something."

I hoped it was one of her famous scones or any kind of baked good. I was hungry. I didn't smell anything appetizing, though, and when she reached into the bag she'd brought, it wasn't baking she brought out but jewelry. I stared. There was a purple stone that I thought was amethyst on a silver chain in her palm. I looked up at her, a question in my eyes.

"It's for protection, dear."

Seeing my continued puzzlement, she said, "Oh, this is awkward, isn't it?"

I didn't want to be rude, but yes, it was, and getting more so by the second. Elspeth took a breath and closed her eyes for a second, then opened them and said, "Did your mother never talk to you about your special abilities?"

I'm sure my mouth dropped wide open. "You know about that?"

How could she know about the ghosts? I'd been so careful. She smiled. "I recognized you right away. We sisters often do, you know."

"Sisters?"

"Sisters, mothers, aunts. Some of us are men, but not so many."

I wasn't going to come right out and say I saw dead people in case this was some kind of test, so I just looked at her. She said again, "Your mother. Didn't she teach you our ways?"

"I never knew my mother."

"Ah, that explains so much." She came deeper into the room and gestured to a pair of armchairs. "Shall we sit?"

I nodded, and we settled. Even though I was anxious to get to Broomewode Hall, I was too curious not to give Elspeth my full attention. She set the pretty necklace on the table, where it winked in the light. "Poppy, have you had odd experiences you couldn't explain? Especially around water?"

I told her about the vision I'd had in the bathtub, where I'd seen the ace of spades dripping blood. "But it was probably fatigue."

She shook her head. "That was the night of the poker game, wasn't it? You foresaw that it was a cutthroat game. Perhaps the blood was a hint that violence was coming."

This was terrible news. "You mean I predicted a murder and then didn't stop it?" I didn't know who was crazier, me or Elspeth.

"No, no," she said quickly. "You couldn't have prevented it, but you felt trouble was coming. And are there things that happen you can't explain?"

Well, if we were two crazy women talking, I might as well tell all. "I see ghosts."

"Really?" As though I was telling her I preferred a marble rolling pin to a wooden one. "And you have no female relatives who share your gift?"

"Gift?" I felt my lip curl. "It's a curse. And I was left in a box on a baker's doorstep when I was a couple of days old.

Any gifted relatives I have, don't seem to have come calling in the last twenty-five years."

"Oh, my poor dear. No wonder you're confused. Well, you've been given great gifts. You simply don't understand how to use them."

"Are you saying there are other people like me?" I wasn't sure if this was good news or the worst ever.

"Oh, yes. We all have different talents, of course, but my dear girl, I believe you are a witch."

I snorted with laughter. Right in Elspeth Peach's face. I didn't mean to, it just came out. "A witch?" I snorted again, but she wasn't laughing along.

She looked perfectly serious and waited until I'd finished my outburst before saying, "It's a great deal to take in, I know. You helped me last night, though, when I shut that dreadful man in the room."

My eyes opened wide. "The door that wouldn't open? That was you?" I'd heard strange mumbling coming from her. I remembered now.

"It wasn't only me, Poppy. It was you, as well. I could feel your power as well as my own." I didn't want to agree, but I thought I knew what she meant.

"I felt like there was a wave of energy and I was part of it. I remember wanting that door to stay closed so Marcus couldn't escape."

"Exactly. We're more powerful when we work together. That's why we have covens."

"Covens," I said faintly. This was more like a fairy tale than a reality show. Or had I drifted onto the wrong set? Instead of featuring on *The Great British Baking Contest,* I was

starring in *Surprise! You're a Witch.* That would actually be a
show I'd like to watch. Not appear on.

She lifted the necklace. "I've put a strong protection spell
on this stone and, as you may know, amethyst is already a
protective crystal. Also, it's associated with water. Very good
for a water witch."

"I'm a water witch?" Now I even had a specialty.

"I believe so."

"And you?" I was having a hard time taking in that the
great Elspeth Peach was a witch.

She chuckled. "I'm an air witch." She rose and fastened
the necklace for me. As it settled over my heart, I felt calmer.
"Try not to take it off."

I put my hand over it. "Protection. Do you think I'm in
danger?"

"Until Gerry's killer is apprehended, I think we should all
be extra careful." She lifted her wrist, and I saw a cluster of
stones in a bracelet. "I'll do my best to keep everyone safe, but
I'm hoping you can help me."

"Me? I've known I was a witch for less than five minutes.
What can I do?"

"Listen to your natural instincts. Settle your mind, and
don't ignore your intuitions. You found Marcus out, didn't
you?"

I was going to say that was just dumb luck, but I remembered how twitchy I'd felt when watching the rushes. I had
found him out. "But any good detective would have done the
same. It was a question of looking."

She smiled at me but didn't argue. "All I ask is that you
stay open. And welcome, little sister." She rose and headed
for the door. Then she turned. "Blessed be."

When she left, I ran to look in the mirror. I wanted to admire the necklace but also look at my own face and see if I looked any different.

The mirror reflected back the same face as always. The necklace was beautiful and looked perfectly ordinary. Whatever power it had was invisible. Still, I was glad to have it, and the walk to Broomewode Hall would give me a chance to go back over our conversation.

Was I really a witch? It would explain how I'd always felt out of place. Even more curious, she'd kept mentioning my mother. Could my real mom have been a witch too? Would I ever learn who she was and why she'd given me away?

Once more, I felt that answers lay at Broomewode Hall.

I'd watched the episode of the baking show where I'd seen the oil painting hanging countless times. I knew every inch of that dining room as well as the poor maid who had to clean it. The enormous bay windows, framed by heavy tapestried curtains woven through with gold. Cream wallpapered walls reaching up to the paneled ceilings, bordered in a deep red runner. The ancient-looking long dining table, in rich mahogany with matching sideboards and display cabinets. The damask-upholstered chairs ready and waiting for the next gala dinner. And then the painting itself. A grand woman, maybe in her early forties, sitting in a large, wicker-backed chair, a woolen shawl draped over her slim shoulders, its pattern the exact match of my baby blanket.

If the police who'd investigated the strange circumstances of my appearance at the bakery, tucked as I was inside the apple box with nothing but that blanket, were right, then the shawl and my blanket had been knitted by hand. Whoever had done that knitting might know something about my mother. And the woman who'd worn it? I wondered if she were still alive. I hoped I'd soon have some answers.

Outside, the air was warmer than I'd expected, a light breeze rustling through the leaves of the whitebeam trees. The tulips and daffodils were magnificent as they tumbled out of their well-manicured flowerbeds, and my lungs filled with crisp, clean air. I'd grabbed an apple from the bowl in the hall so I could avoid seeing anyone at breakfast, though I guessed everybody was exhausted from last night and sleeping in. Strangely, though, I didn't feel tired. In fact, it was as though caffeine was coursing through my veins that morning. I set off for the manor house with gusto, more determined than I think I'd ever been in my life—including when I had to practice making puff pastry for the show. Lady Frome could be as elusive as she wanted, but I was going to get into that building and get some answers.

I wandered over the footbridge and stared down into the stream. Water witch? Really? I touched the crystal at my throat. Sure, I'd always been drawn to water, but so were lots of people. I was clearly odd, though. Instead of fighting the water witch idea, I wondered if Elspeth could be right.

There was movement in the water. Fish, I thought, leaning over and peering closer. The surface of the water began to ripple. Did the fish think I'd come with food? I imagined greedy mouths searching the surface for crumbs. Then the surface stilled as suddenly as it had rippled, and a chill came over me. As though I were watching a grainy old black and white movie or a newsreel, I saw the image of a woman.

I couldn't see her face, only the back of her. She was running, but awkwardly, as though she were carrying something heavy that was slowing her down. She wore a baggy dress, and her long, dark hair trailed behind her as she ran. I could feel waves of sadness and fear coming from her. My heart was pounding. She ran across a grass field that could be anywhere, and then she ran across a footbridge—this footbridge, I was sure of it, not because the bridge itself was particularly unique, but I knew it deep inside myself. On the other side of the bridge, she turned to look back, and I saw that she wasn't carrying anything but a cloth bag over her shoulder. She'd been running awkwardly because she was heavily pregnant.

Her face was in shadow, but her belly was too prominent to miss. She had her hands wrapped around the bump in a protective way. Then she turned and continued her flight.

The stream was once again a stream. I stood there for a long time staring down, but nothing else happened, except I grew chilled. I walked to the end of the bridge, where the woman in my vision had turned. Sure enough, there was a good view of Broomewode Hall from there. She'd have looked back and seen the upper windows, mainly, and the peaks of the roof.

What had that young woman been running from? I didn't ask myself who she was because I thought I knew. She'd been my mother.

CHAPTER 12

*I*t was easy to find the front entrance to the manor house: Two great stone pillars flanked the enormous double doors. It looked like the mouth to Hades in the books I'd read while studying Persephone's myth for my sponge challenge. I swallowed hard and reminded myself this wasn't the entrance to the afterlife, just that of the British upper classes. How bad could it be?

The turrets stood proudly against the pale blue sky. They were grand and imperious. Approaching the great house from its imposing entrance, I was in awe. I was also afraid—what if Benedict, that strange sword-wielding guy, was on patrol again this morning? Was that his weird job around here? Scare away the tourists? I'd better not waste a minute. I picked up the pace.

In the distance to my left was the wide white canopy of the baking tent, devoid now of the hustle and bustle of the filming crew. There was police tape around it, and a small team of technicians were combing the area for clues, presumably. I had no idea if next week's filming would go ahead. If

Donald Friesen had anything to do with it, though, we'd be back creaming sugar and butter, carrying on as normal. He was the very epitome of the phrase *the show must go on!* But that particular question mark hanging above the series would have to wait for an answer. I had more important things to think about than a lemon posset.

I walked up the gravel path to the entrance. Either side, the perfectly groomed grounds looked like striped green carpet, rolled out, waiting for someone far more glamorous than me to arrive. I was determined not to feel intimidated, yet my stomach was flipping like a pancake. From what I'd gleaned about Lady Frome, she was a woman not to be trifled with. I knew that she'd been reluctant to be involved in the baking show in the first place. I imagined, like many old British families with sprawling estates, the family needed a cash influx to keep their estate running.

Deeply private and wary of the cameras, Lady Frome had come across as haughty and privileged. She'd looked like an extraordinarily elegant woman, classic in her dress. She was tall and added to her height with slim heels that clicked as she walked along the flagstone corridors, pointing out priceless antiques with a polished fingernail. She was imperious and the very picture of British aristocracy. At the mere thought of her, I trembled in my American boots.

After what seemed an age, I reached the carriage drive and stepped into the portico entrance. Even the front door was a work of art. The wooden panels were carved with swirling patterns, and a brass knocker in the shape of a lion's head took center stage. It was about the same size as a real lion's head. To my shame, I noticed that my hands were trembling. How could I be scared when yesterday I'd come face-to-face with a dead body? I took a deep breath and knocked. *Get it together, Poppy. You've got this.*

After the sound of the knocker, it was deathly silent. All I could hear were the birds tweeting their morning songs. No footsteps. Nothing echoing along the corridor. Dare I knock again? I glanced to my right, and hanging from the top of the porch was a circular brass plate with a thick red rope attached. What a doofus. Of course, no one would hear a knocker in this vast house. The lion's head was purely for show. I pulled on the rope, and a crashing bell chimed, and a semicircular fanlight above my head blinked on. I had the strange sensation that I was being watched. I stood back and saw that there were two tiny cameras hidden in the ivy that graced the top of the portico. They were pointing directly at me. I gulped. Maybe whoever was watching had taken one look at my very ordinary appearance and decided that it wasn't worth the bother to open the door. I fussed with my hair and stood a little straighter. I'd never carried breath mints in my life, but I longed for one now.

A few moments later, the door slowly opened, and a portly gentleman dressed in a formal black jacket and striped trousers stared back at me. His shirt was impossibly white and starched so severely that it stood almost at angles around his broad neck.

"May I help you?" he asked, giving me a decidedly unimpressed once over. I'd already decided on an alias even before that strange vision of a woman running away from Broomewode Hall. I didn't want news of my visit to the Hall getting back to the production, since I was blatantly ignoring the rules. I'd decided to become Tabitha Worth, a location scout from LA hoping to feature Broomewode Hall in an upcoming movie. Lots of cash and very few scenes was what I'd promise. I hoped that would get me a tour of the place.

"Good morning. I'm Tabitha Worth," I said. "I'm here to inquire..." But before I could finish, a gentleman I recognized from that same behind-the-scenes episode of the Baking Contest came to the door behind the butler. Lord Frome wore a tweed jacket, brown slacks and a matching tweed flat cap perched at a jaunty angle on top of his head. He looked like a cardboard cutout of the aristocracy. A golden Labrador was by his side, and—alarmingly—a rifle was tucked under his left arm.

He stared at me and seemed to recoil, as if something about my face was hideous or misshapen. I wiped at my cheek and mouth in case I'd accidentally smeared anything there. There was an uncomfortable moment's silence as the three of us stood awkwardly until the dog bounded over to me and jumped up for some attention. I bent down to his level and petted him. "Hello there," I said. "What a handsome boy you are." His paws scrabbled at my legs. I tickled him behind the ears.

The butler introduced me as Tabitha Worth. Before I could explain about the fictitious movie deal, Lord Frome said, "Of course. You're here for the Assistant Cook's position. My dear wife is at her wit's end. Our cook is indisposed. She's never gone off sick before." He sounded as though an ill servant was a serious inconvenience to him. "Tilbury, if you see my son, tell him to join us clay pigeon shooting."

Before I could reply, Lord Frome strode out into the grounds, the dog bounding joyfully ahead. I saw them heading for an old battered Land Rover, which had been parked a little way from the main path.

The butler said, "Wait here, Miss Worth," and he gestured me inside, pointing at an uncomfortable-looking bench beside a long trestle table. He walked away with purpose, his footsteps light and elegant for a man of his size. At least now I knew why Katie Donegal hadn't met with me. She was ill. I hoped it wasn't anything serious.

As soon as the butler was out of sight, I leapt to my feet, almost knocking over a huge porcelain vase of fragrant pink lilies. I surveyed my surroundings. A dusty-looking chandelier poorly lighted the hall. The paneling on the walls seemed to suck up any light that came in through the leaden windows. Although grand, there was an element of faded glory about the place. In the corner was a suit of armor that looked in need of a polish. The wallpapered walls with their sumptuous swirling patterns were peeling a little in the cracks between strips. I'd read about how many old country estates in Britain were struggling, particularly those built in the Georgian era. It must have been difficult for Lord and Lady Frome to open up their home to the TV show and various weddings held throughout the year. They were notoriously private and worked hard to keep people like me out. Not for the first time, I wondered if the Champneys had something to hide.

I crept along the corridor. I'd no idea how long it might take the butler to find Lady Frome in this vast house. I couldn't even guess how many rooms there were. What must it feel like to live in a place like this? How could anyone keep track of their belongings? Or each other? And staff wasn't as cheap as it had been two hundred years ago, so it must be a constant struggle to keep the place up.

I thought longingly again of my darling little cottage. The

Olde Bakery, with its homey kitchen—complete with Mildred the ghost—and misshapen rooms that were so comfortable and cozy. Despite Broomewode's grandeur, I wouldn't trade places with Lord and Lady Frome.

I wanted to find the dining room where the oil painting of my blanket was hanging, but the corridor was long and wide, with a series of closed doors either side. Which one was the dining room? I could hear a woman's voice coming closer, although what was being said was unclear. I hurried back to my bench, smoothed down my hair, pressed my knees and ankles together like a proper lady, and waited.

Lady Frome appeared at the top of the grand staircase. Gone were the jeans and cashmere sweater I'd seen her in yesterday. Instead, she was wearing an outfit more similar to those I'd seen on the show: navy slacks and a white silk shirt, two strings of pearls wound around her delicate throat. She was certainly a striking woman.

She walked down the stairs and came toward me then raised one eyebrow as if waiting for me to stand in her presence. I did, feeling like a bad servant, and introduced myself, giving my alias once more.

"And you're here for the assistant cook job, are you? Where's your CV?" She held out her hand for my resume looking impatient.

All of a sudden, I lost the nerve to pretend I was a movie location scout. If she asked me any questions, I'd fall to pieces. Instead, I decided to go with the truth. "I'm not here for a job. I'm looking for someone who may have worked here—her name was Valerie." I only had a demented old woman's word that Valerie was my mother's name, but it was a start.

Did Lady Frome's face stiffen? I thought so, but it was a momentary impression.

She gave me a withering look. Clearly, I had let her down not being an eager, fully qualified cook with years of experience.

"How on earth would I recall a servant who worked here decades ago?" she said. "We're on high security alert after a suspicious death last night. You should never have been allowed inside the house." She raised her voice. "Tilbury?"

The butler reappeared so quickly, he must have been hovering within earshot.

"Please show this woman out. Through the servants' door."

With that, she turned on her heels and went back the way she had come. But suddenly she stopped and glanced over her shoulder at me. I waited, breath held. "I am sorry I can't help you," she said eventually. And with that, she climbed the rest of the grand stairs and disappeared from view.

For a moment, I thought I saw a shadow moving at the top of the landing, but I couldn't be sure. Had someone else been there the whole time? A spirit perhaps? Broomewode Hall was ancient, and there had to be many generations of spirits lingering within its walls. I hoped they weren't too restless. There didn't seem to be a lot of love and understanding in this house.

Well, despite the somewhat rude dismissal, Lady Frome had given me some information. She'd said she couldn't be expected to remember a woman who'd worked there decades earlier. But I hadn't given any idea of the timeframe. While that didn't prove she'd lied about knowing Valerie, it was definitely interesting.

By sending me out the servants' door, she'd meant to show me my place, but she'd also given me a chance to do some more snooping. I was delighted to have an excuse to go to the servants' quarters, even if that meant forgoing a trip to the dining room and examining the painting up close. Tilbury silently escorted me along the hallway, into a long, narrow corridor, and then pointed in the direction of some steep stairs. "You can exit via the kitchen, Miss Worth," he said. "Please don't disrupt the staff. They are preparing luncheon for Lord Frome and his guests."

Right. The clay pigeon shooters.

The scent of stewing spiced meat hit me before I even opened the door. The sound of pots and pans clanging and the warmth of a busy kitchen enveloped me as I entered. Broomewode Hall might be hundreds of years old, but this kitchen was modern. A woman was standing by the industrial-sized stove stirring an enormous pot. A young woman was also busy chopping vegetables. I recognized her as the Italian girl who'd sent me away yesterday. To my surprise, the woman stirring the pot was Eve from the inn's pub.

"Eve?" I asked.

She turned and smiled at me. "Poppy. I've had to lend a hand today as poor Katie's broken her arm." She gave me a humorous look and beckoned with her chin to where an older woman with curly gray hair was directing a young girl in the correct way to peel potatoes. "Go and talk to her. Please."

I felt like an extra in *Downton Abbey* as I walked over to the cook, her right arm in a cast, who was obviously having a hard time giving up control of her kingdom. At last. This was

Katie Donegal. She wasn't much taller than five feet and quite round.

However, when I introduced myself, her green eyes were wide and kind. She took me to a sitting room off the kitchen, and sighed as she sat down. She rubbed her cast and apologized for not being able to see me the day before, but she'd broken her arm on the way to meet me, in fact. "I tripped over a tree root, I was in that much of a hurry. But how nice to meet you, dear," she said with a soft Irish brogue. "How can I be helping you?"

I wasn't sure how to start. "Did Eve tell you about me?"

"Oh, Poppy, yes, of course. One of the lucky bakers. Though I suppose you don't feel so lucky after all this terrible business last night. Do you know what happened? Everyone here has been gossiping like crazy. They're very worried, having a dead body on their grounds. What if they stop the filming?" She glanced around and then dropped her voice, even though we were alone. "They rely on the money, you know. And I imagine it helps pay my salary as well. Also, I've always wondered if that Jonathon is as dishy in real life as he is on screen. But look, I'm blathering on. As usual. Eve said you wanted to ask me about some local history. You can make me a cup of tea while you do. I'm useless without my right hand. Useless."

I put the kettle on. There was a teapot, tea, instant coffee and even a jar of cookies. A small jug of milk had been set out. I wondered whether it was Eve's idea to try and keep Katie Donegal in here as much as possible and out of the kitchen.

"Do you know anything about this death?" she asked

avidly. She was a natural gossip, and I suspected that without her busy job, boredom was taking its toll.

I told Katie that I didn't know much about what happened yesterday, only that the police were deep into an investigation. She was about to ask me more questions, but I worried Lady Frome would somehow find out I was loitering and have me thrown out, so I said, "Katie, I need to ask you about a woman named Valerie. I think she may have worked at Broomewode Hall or maybe lived close by. Eve told me you know everyone around here. Does that name sound familiar?"

Her kind face grew suddenly sad and also wary. "I think that tea's brewed long enough," she said, turning me back to my tea-making duties. By the time I'd added the amount of milk and sugar she directed and handed her a shortbread, she was back in control. "What did you say the name was again?"

"Valerie."

"No last name, then?"

"No. I was hoping you might be able to help."

"Oh, well, we've had a lot of girls through here over the years." She glanced at me, and I felt there was an inner struggle going on. Finally, she said, "I believe there was a young woman of that name. It would be more than twenty years ago now at least. But she left. I wish I could tell you more, but she wasn't here very long. I never got to know her well."

"Do you think you could find her last name?"

She shook her head. "There'd be no reason to keep records going that far back."

"Do you know where she came from?"

"I'm sorry, dear. It's so long ago. I don't think she was local."

"Did she leave a forwarding address?" I'd pinned so many hopes on this interview, and I was getting nowhere.

I thought she'd remembered something. She leaned forward and looked at me intently. "She didn't. I remember that she left without a word to anyone. Sometimes, people don't want to be found. It's kinder to respect their wishes."

I was about to ask whether this mysterious Valerie who seemed to arrive from nowhere and vanish into thin air, had been pregnant when a male voice could be heard from the kitchen. Tilbury, probably, about to drag me to the dungeon for not scampering out the servants' door as I'd been ordered.

But the man who appeared in Katie's doorway was the one I'd first met yesterday. He wasn't wearing an old-fashioned dress or sword now. His jeans were modern, and he wore them with boots and a heavy navy blue sweater. In my experience, ghosts didn't have extensive wardrobes. Whatever they died in was usually what they were stuck wearing. Which meant that my ghost probably wasn't a ghost after all.

He was holding a bouquet of flowers, clearly intended for the injured cook, but when he saw me, he jolted to a stop. I felt like I'd been caught doing something wrong, but this wasn't feudal times. Katie was allowed to have visitors. Before I could say anything, Katie launched into a speech. "Oh, Lord Winford. Are those for me? I feel such a fool. Fell over like a clumsy oaf, and my arm snapped like a twig."

"Katie, don't get formal on me now. It's always been Ben, and it always will be."

"You're not a little boy anymore. Oh, and you did look lovely in your ceremonial robes. How's the painting coming?

Lady Frome was right. It will look lovely hanging in the long gallery with the rest of your ancestors."

Aha. At least now I understood why he'd been dressed so strangely that first day. Lord Winford might be many things, but he was clearly no ghost.

Katie seemed both pleased and flustered by his visit. "This young lady was keeping me company. She's with the baking show, you know. Quite a celebrity."

"Yes. Poppy Wilkinson. We've met." He didn't look thrilled to see me, but he didn't look like he was going to call the cops on me for trespassing, either. Nor was he surprised that I was a show contestant. He must have checked up on me after our last meeting, if you could call it that. He put the vase of flowers on the table near Katie's elbow. If she was getting a visit from his lordship, I'd better make myself scarce.

"It was so nice visiting with you, Katie," I said. "I hope your arm heals soon."

"Thank you, my dear. And remember what I said." Translated to American, what she'd said was *Butt out!*

I nodded to Lord Winford and made to move past him. Up close, he had intense dark eyes and his dark, curly hair had a leaf caught in it. He must have picked those flowers himself. In spite of myself, I was charmed that he'd bring flowers to the cook. No doubt he'd done that instead of shooting clay pigeons.

Our gazes caught. "Give me a minute, Katie. I'll see Poppy out."

I was going to tell him not to bother, but he was already striding ahead of me.

In truth, it wasn't so easy to find the servants' exit. We turned twice down narrow hallways.

"It's a bit of a rabbit warren," he said, as we finally approached the door I'd knocked on only yesterday. He clearly couldn't get me out of there fast enough. He swung the door open with a flourish and said, "Here you are."

I stepped out onto the set of stone stairs and was about to say goodbye and get on my way when he said, "You did read the rules, didn't you? Show contestants aren't allowed on this part of the property."

"Yes, Your Lordship." Okay, I went a bit heavy on the title, but then anyone who wandered the garden dressed in scarlet robes begged to be treated with sarcasm. However, I was going to be in serious trouble if he reported me to the production people. Once more, I decided to stick with the truth as much as I dared.

Before I got into the whole Valerie thing, I heard a familiar mew. "Gateau!" I said as she pushed herself against my calf. "What are you doing all the way up here?" I had a sudden terrible thought: What if Gateau was Lady Frome's cat? "She isn't the family pet, is she?" I asked Lord Winford with trepidation. I couldn't stand the thought of that cold woman anywhere near my sweet girl.

"Goodness, no. We're dog people, and she doesn't look tough enough to be a mouser."

I picked up Gateau and faced him. "The truth is, I'm looking for someone who may have worked here some years ago. A relative."

"I wish you the best of luck. But I'd urge you to remember: there's nothing more complicated in life than family dynamics. You may well end up wishing you hadn't bothered."

And with that parting shot, he closed the door.

CHAPTER 13

By the time I arrived back at the inn, disheartened and frustrated, it was lunchtime. Gateau scampered off in the direction of the inn's little garden, but I had the feeling she'd be back soon. In fact, I felt strongly that the cat would be there in a flash if I needed her.

I touched my hand to the amethyst around my neck. Elspeth had suggested I had a witch's powers, and I wondered if there was some kind of spell that would help me get the answers I needed. So far, all my 'gift' seemed to give me was visits from the departed and disturbing daydreams. Lucky me.

The dining room was busy. Everyone still here was tucking into full plates and talking over the noise of scraping cutlery. As I walked in, Florence stood up and put both hands to her breast. "Where have you been? I've been so worried. I went to fetch you for breakfast, but there was no answer. I didn't even have your mobile number."

I hadn't considered that anyone would worry about my safety. I was touched. I apologized and told her that I'd gone for a long walk around the grounds to clear my head. I realized I'd left my phone in my room, which was pretty stupid considering there was an unsolved murder in the area, though I suspected the killer was in custody. I still couldn't believe that uptight Marcus Hoare had killed Gerry.

I ran up to fetch it, then I plugged my number into Florence's mobile phone, and she saved it under my name with a little gold star emoji. It was very sweet. When she sent me her number, I added a tiny cake emoji.

"I'm just glad you're safe," Florence said. "No one has seen Marcus this morning, so I think he's being held by the police. I can't believe he's suspected of murder! It's crazy that people think he could do something like that. I just don't understand it." She was almost on the brink of tears. It must be the drama student in her, feeding on all the theatrics. Why was she so upset about Marcus? I felt reassured. At least we knew who the culprit was.

I ordered quiche and salad for lunch and a large coffee, as I hadn't fancied the instant stuff in Katie's room.

Florence patted the chair beside her, and I joined her, Maggie and Hamish as they ate. Maggie placed her hand on mine. "You gave us all quite the fright, dear," she said. She lowered her voice. "Please don't disappear like that again." Elspeth could have told them I was safe, but Elspeth wasn't there. I was so touched that they'd worried about me. In spite of the tragedy, or because of it, we were bonding.

Another diner entered the room, and I choked on my coffee when I saw it was Marcus. He glared at all of us. "Here I am back. You'd better all run screaming." The room fell silent. His face was pallid, and his usual perfectly Brylcreem-styled hair was in disarray. The dark circles that had appeared under his eyes last night were now almost purple in hue. He'd been through the wringer, that was for sure. I was stunned. After discovering how he'd tampered with the ovens, I'd certainly not expected to see him back anytime soon. Or ever again. Surely he had to be responsible for Gerry's electric shock—whether it was on purpose or an accident.

After a moment, Hamish piped up. "So, they've released you then, mate." His tone was light, but the implication of his words hung heavy in the air.

"Of course, they've released me," Marcus replied. "It was an absolute joke they took me in for questioning in the first place." He stopped, crossed his arms and looked around the room defiantly. "I'm starving." He went to an empty table and sat by himself. No one resumed conversation. Instead, we watched as he ordered a steak sandwich and a beer. Still no one spoke.

Finally, he burst out with, "Look. I don't owe anyone an explanation."

More silence.

"But since you're all so set on lavishing me with this ridiculous attention...I suppose I should tell you that there was nothing I could say that helped the police investigation. They asked me all kinds of absurd questions for what seemed like hours. But I had no answers. I had no idea what they were trying to get at half the time. I'm a banker, not a murderer."

I should have kept my mouth shut, but I knew what I'd seen on those rushes. I wasn't buying his innocent act. "But you did tamper with Gerry's oven, didn't you? And I'm sure you put salt in his sugar for the tarte au citron challenge."

Marcus glared at me with loathing. "I had nothing to do with Gerry's death whatsoever." He stopped again, ran a hand through his messy hair and then smoothed down his wrinkled shirt. "But there *is* something I'm going to confess. Since the police know now, it'll come out soon anyway."

Everyone waited, but I knew exactly what he was going to say.

"I did know Gerry before the show."

There was a collective gasp. "What?" Florence said. She was pink-faced, a flush spreading down her neck, her eyes lively. I wondered again if she might be enjoying the drama. It also seemed like Marcus relished being the center of attention. What was wrong with everyone? How could this be exciting to them? A fellow baker was dead.

"I'll tell you all what I told the police. Gerry did a renovation on my house last year. But that wasn't the only thing he did. Turns out, our Gerry had quite the penchant for other people's property. Like my wife."

He stopped. Took a sip of his beer, picked up his knife and fork and put them down again. "From the moment we began filming, I couldn't believe my bad luck. The whole reason I'd come onto the show was to take my mind off my divorce, and here was the man who caused it. He slept with my wife, destroyed my marriage and overcharged on the renovation. So yes, I sabotaged his sponge. I put salt in his sugar. I burnt his pie." He said these things with relish, as though he was proud of himself. "I'd do it all again, too. I enjoyed humiliating him the way he'd humiliated me. But I did not kill him." He speared a french fry. "And you might all be interested to know that someone else will soon be sitting in my chair at the police station. I overheard them talking.

The unlucky fellow should be grateful that I warmed that interview chair for him."

Everyone looked around the room. Who could Marcus possibly be talking about? Maggie raised her eyebrows at me and shook her head. Florence was already stress-eating the chips off Hamish's plate. "Well, goodness, that was quite the show," she whispered. "If only he baked as well as he acted, perhaps he'd have a chance of winning."

"No possibility of that now, I'm afraid," Maggie said. "The judges won't put up with sabotage. Marcus will have to go."

"I'm not sorry to say goodbye to him," Florence whispered back. "What kind of man sabotages another man's pie?"

"One who's hurting," Hamish said. "Being in pain can make us do funny things. Terrible things." He shook his head and sipped from his mug of tea.

Marcus was cutting his steak into neat squares. Donald Friesen joined him. I could see the conversation wasn't a friendly one. Donald's hands were flat on the table, and he was leaning forward. I couldn't hear the words, but the body language and tone were both angry.

Maggie said, "This show is a national treasure. The concept came from the village fete, you know, originally, where people are judged on their marmalades or their tea buns. The Great British Baking Contest is good clean fun and not the place to take out personal vendettas on television." She looked very upset. "I don't want to be part of the cast that broke a national treasure!"

As though he'd heard her, Marcus hung his head and clasped his hands together, almost in supplication.

Donald abruptly stood, realizing we were all watching. He was back to his usual smartly dressed self. Silver cufflinks glinted in his pressed white shirt, and he was wearing a tan linen suit. But his face was as white as a sheet, and those stress lines on his forehead hadn't gone anywhere. "Listen up, everyone," he said. "I hope you've had a good night's sleep, and thank you all for your patience while we process this terrible, terrible tragedy."

He smiled at us and continued to explain that the production team was doing everything it could to help the police, but the show was currently under review. The room was momentarily stunned into silence. My stomach dropped, and a wave of despair washed over me. I'd come so far, hours and hours of practice baking, going through my audition hundreds of times with Gina and finally getting on the show. And this morning I'd actually managed to get into the manor house. In spite of what Katie Donegal had said, I was convinced Broomewode Hall, the mysterious Valerie and my mother were connected. I was convinced that there were answers about my past hidden inside Broomewode Hall. If they suspended this season of the Great British Baking Contest, I'd have no reason to hang around. This was terrible news.

Then the questions from all the contestants erupted. Donald dealt with them like a consummate professional, batting concerns away with smooth catchphrases and pearls of PR wisdom. He told us if it were up to him, the show would go on, no two ways about it. He was fighting in our corner, of course he was, but ultimately the decision was out of his hands. It lay with his superiors, and he was confident that they'd evaluate all that happened here and come up with the best solution for everyone concerned.

And that's when I saw him. My latest ghost.

The familiar shadowy line. A hazy rim around the edges. The faded expression. This one wasn't wearing royal robes. He was wearing a red shirt patterned with trucks and cars, dark trousers and on his feet brilliant white running shoes.

Gerry!

I was so startled I spoke his name at the same moment I gasped. This caused me to choke on my coffee and burst into a horrendous coughing fit. Hamish passed me a glass of water and slapped me on the back. It took every single ounce of self-control I had to arrange my face into something resembling normal. Gerry was standing by the window, surveying the room, arms folded across his chest. He looked distinctly peeved. And tired. Well, I guessed he'd had a long journey.

He was scanning the room suspiciously when his eyes rested on me. I couldn't help it. I looked right back at him. He blinked several times, and then his eyebrows shot up and he mouthed, "Poppy?" at me.

Poor Gerry, of course he was a restless spirit. He'd been struck down in his prime. Murdered.

My eyes had nearly stopped watering and I'd dared another sip of coffee when Sergeant Lane walked in. He was wearing a somber gray shirt and black trousers, and he looked as tired as everyone else in the room. He greeted the room with a small, professional smile and headed to where some of the crew was eating and talking. The room went quiet again. He laid a hand on Aaron Keel's shoulder. Aaron had a mouth full of fish pie, and he turned to face Sergeant Lane, still chewing. He swallowed hard when he saw who the hand belonged to.

A low exchange followed that I couldn't quite hear. And I wasn't the only one trying to listen. I wondered if this had something to do with the ovens or with the poker game. I remembered then how Marcus had told Gina and I that Aaron was furious about losing the poker game. What was the phrase he'd used to describe it? *Gerry took so much cash off of him...he's lucky he made it out in one piece.* Aaron had a stinking temper on him, I'd seen it myself.

Aaron stood up. To the crew, he said, "Don't worry, lads, I'm just helping the police with their enquiries." He followed the sergeant out of the room. There was something a little too self-confident in the way he walked, too assured. It was the polar opposite of Marcus's little showdown last night, but in a way, it was worse. What kind of person remained that calm under that kind of pressure?

If a police officer asked me to accompany him to the station, no matter how squeaky-clean I might be, I'd still be freaking out.

Everyone burst into chatter the minute he was out of sight. We were unanimously shocked. Aaron was in charge of the ovens, and he'd checked Gerry's and told him it was working fine. Was he crappy at his job? Or had he decided to teach Gerry a poker lesson he'd never forget?

Gerry, meanwhile, was doing everything in his power to draw my attention. Honestly, he was like a two-year-old. He'd discovered that having no earthly body, gravity didn't have the same effect. He was currently walking up the curtains.

"Guys," I said, addressing the table. "I'm going to go back to my room for a bit. Have a quick shower. I'll see you back here later."

I left the table before anyone could reply and walked over to the window. Gerry slid down the curtains with a whoop only I could hear. I nodded my head discreetly to indicate that he should follow me. He stared at me incredulously but did as I asked. I led the way and waited till we got upstairs and I'd opened the door before I spoke in the soothing tone I'd adopted for ghosts.

"Gerry. Please don't be concerned. I'm here to help you. I have this special gift. I can see people once they've passed." I stopped. What if he didn't know that he'd passed over? "Wait, you do know that you're dead, right?"

"Of course, I do! I'm furious. One minute I was in the tent checking the oven, and the next: BOOM. Bright lights. Flashing colors. Then this. A weird floaty feeling and no one can bloomin' hear or see me. Except for you. My sweet pal Poppy, who, it turns out, sees ghosts." He gave a dramatic shrug and shook his head. "It just gets weirder and weirder." He jumped onto the bed. "Nice room," he said, looking around. "Bigger than mine."

"Is that all you remember, Gerry? The flash and bang?"

"Yes. It was a shock. What happened to me?"

Carefully and slowly, I explained to Gerry that he'd been electrocuted. We didn't yet know what exactly had caused the electric shock, if it'd been a faulty oven or if someone had tampered with the controls. I told him that the police were investigating his death as suspicious and that everyone had been interviewed. Marcus had been forced to admit that he'd known Gerry and admitted sabotaging his baking.

"I knew it! What did I tell you? I would *never* undercook a sponge. And my tarte, ruined by that fiend. Then he even burned my final pie. Oh, I'll get him if it's the last thing I do."

"Gerry, Marcus was retaliating against you for sleeping with his wife. Remember?" I didn't add the obvious. Gerry had already done the last thing he'd ever do. Life as he'd known it was over. "Marcus swears he didn't kill you."

"Hmm. Nice of him."

Gerry began to amuse himself by running his hands through solid objects. "Hah, Pop, look at this," he said, pushing his head and torso through the wall. I rolled my eyes. This was not my first ghost story. I guessed it was his, though. When he pulled his head back into the room, he said, "That was cool. Donald was in the hall talking to Elspeth and Jonathon. Seems like Marcus is going to invent a work emergency and pull out of the competition."

"So it's going ahead then?"

He shrugged, and the cars and trucks on his red shirt all took a short ride. "For the rest of you, maybe."

He tried to lift my hairbrush and looked peeved when his hands slid right through the brush.

"Do you think it could have been an accident?" I asked him. "Even if Marcus was sabotaging your baking, I suppose you could still have a faulty oven."

Gerry stopped trying to pick things up and turned to me. "No. I might have got a shock, but for full-on electrocution, I reckon someone clipped something like jumper cables to a metal piece of the oven and attached the other end to the electric panel. All I had to do was touch the handle and I'd be fried like crispy bacon. Once I was dead, they turned the power off, unhooked the cable and walked away."

"The police are interviewing Aaron now."

"Well, he's the logical culprit. He's the electrician, and he was pretty annoyed that I took all the winnings at poker. But would he really kill me over a few hundred quid?"

I shrugged. Right now I had no idea what to think. None of this made sense. "Your money's missing from your wallet."

"What?" He appeared outraged. "Murdering me wasn't enough? They had to steal from me too?"

My phone started ringing. "I'll get it," Gerry joked as his hand passed through my phone.

I put my hand through the cold patch where he stood and picked up my phone. I heard Florence's soft velvety voice and breathed a sigh of relief. She told me that Donald was gathering everybody downstairs to talk about the show. She urged me to join them.

I turned back to Gerry, who was sitting cross-legged on top of the chest of drawers. "I see everyone is more interested in baking than solving my murder."

"Don't worry, Gerry," I said. "I promise you that I'll get to the bottom of this. The police are doing everything they can. You saw them take Aaron down to the station. They'll question him about the ovens, and we'll find out more soon. We were a great team in life. We'll be a great team after it."

Even he had to smile at that. He went to high-five me, but his hand disappeared through mine.

I had to give him credit: Gerry was coping remarkably well. I couldn't be seen talking to thin air, so I told Gerry to stay put, not peek through my things (I was thinking particularly of my underwear drawer) and generally avoid causing any mischief. If there was one thing I knew about ghosts, it was that they didn't lose their past personalities. Gerry would be just as cheeky as he had been yesterday morning. I didn't feel especially confident that he'd listen to me and stay here, but what choice did I have? I had to appeal to his better, ghostly nature. I told him that I would join the others down-stairs and report back later.

I made it to the dining room just as a woman who turned out to be Donald's boss and a network executive began to speak. I hadn't met her before. Her tall, willowy frame was wrapped in a black jumpsuit, and large gold hoops peeked out beneath her brown bobbed hair. She spoke with a broad Northern accent, and as I walked in, she was telling everyone how sorry she was that such a tragedy had occurred during what should have been a fun and enjoyable experience. The whole TV station was aghast at what had happened and was hoping for a quick investigation so that Gerry's family could have some much-needed answers. After a long night's discussion with all involved in the making of the show, it had been decided that the series would continue. Filming would be delayed by seven days, and the series would be dedicated to Gerry's memory.

They hoped that any gossip surrounding what had happened on the show would be long forgotten by the time it aired, and she urged all of us not to speak to the press or report back to our families before the police finished their investigation.

She said there was nothing worse for Gerry's family than idle gossip and that it would be a terrible shame for a show that was such a well-loved institution to suffer at the sharp tongue of the press. She thanked everyone for her patience.

The room erupted into chatter. Clearly everyone was pleased at what had been decided. Although I felt bad for Gerry, I was immensely relieved that my search for my birth parents could continue. In fact, I was more determined than ever. With all the strange things happening around here, knowing about my heritage was becoming urgent.

I wanted to understand more about myself, whether seeing ghosts was something which had been passed down to me through generations of my family. I turned to look for Florence, knowing that she'd be over the moon at the network's decision, but who did I see instead, but Gerry, standing in the doorway with that cheeky grin on his face. He looked at me and then stretched up toward the ceiling, levitating off of the ground, and I got a flash of his pale, round stomach.

When he saw Marcus, he looked as annoyed as a ghost can. He marched over to where Marcus stood, alone at the back. Gerry wound his arm back like a star pitcher and took a tremendous swing, punching his rival in the gut. I winced in sympathy, but Marcus was oblivious as Gerry's arm thrust out his back. After that, I watched as Gerry ran at him from across the room, jumped on Marcus, dropped on him from the ceiling, even hooked his arms, stood behind and garroted the man who'd sabotaged his baking. He wasn't doing Marcus any harm, and maybe it helped get his irritation out of his system. After a while, Marcus shivered and buttoned up his coat. Gerry pretended to be a wild dog and growled, then snapped at Marcus's nose. He looked over at me and rubbed his hands together as if to say, job done. He was going to be a troublesome sidekick, that much was certain.

$\mathcal{E}$veryone dispersed when the network executive finished talking, but we still weren't allowed to go home. I didn't mind. I needed more time to continue my search *and* I wanted to help solve Gerry's murder. But I tried to make it seem like I was as aggrieved as everyone else was and threw in some whines and moans. If there's one thing I've learned that the British love, it's complaining.

To my delight, Eve was back. She said lunch at the big house had gone fine, but the sooner Katie was out of her cast and back in charge of her kitchen, the better for everyone.

Of course, the electrocuted baker was the hot topic of conversation at Broomewode Hall as well as here. There'd never been such a scandal in this quiet, rural part of Somerset. Everyone at the Hall, from the clay-pigeon-shooting guests to the kitchen helpers, was terribly upset.

I was listening to Eve, trying to console her, when I realized Gerry had ignored my wishes to go back upstairs and instead followed me to the bar. He leaned on its sticky surface, gazing at Eve. "Oof, I could murder a pint right about now," he said, watching Eve pull a beer. I shot him a furious look and ignored him. Eve kept lamenting Gerry's death. Turns out, she'd thought he was quite handsome, in a naughty-school-boy kind of way. Gerry wolf-whistled. "Missed an opportunity there." I was about to reply when I caught myself and clapped a hand over my mouth. I never had this problem with Mildred at home in my kitchen. I was going to have to get used to having an audience.

I continued to ignore him. Maybe Gerry was going to be more of a hindrance than a help.

"It's nice someone's sorry I'm gone," Gerry said to me, pointedly. Oh, poor Gerry. I hadn't had any real experience dealing with recent ghosts. All the ones I'd encountered were already used to their fate and getting on with their business. I couldn't even imagine how confused and hurt he must be right now. But neither could I explain how much I cared in front of Eve, unless I wanted to end up in an institution. I glowered at Gerry. "Okay okay," he said, hands up, and walked out of the bar.

"And how did you get on with Katie?" Eve asked.

I told her how unhelpful Katie Donegal had been, and she wrinkled her brow. "That's not like Katie. I'd have sworn she knew every girl who ever worked in her kitchen. She loves to talk, but she's kind, too, and was always hearing about their troubles and heartaches. If there was a girl in the kitchen Katie didn't know much about, she must have been very reserved indeed."

Or Katie was lying. I had no idea why, but I'd sensed there was a lot she wasn't telling me.

"Ben brought Katie flowers while you were there, and he escorted you out. He's a good lad." She shot me a glance.

"He'll inherit all of it, you know, and be the Earl of Frome himself one of these days."

I hoped he'd learn some better manners than his parents had demonstrated. Though taking flowers to an injured cook did suggest he was a better man than his father. "Katie called him Lord Winwood." I'd been confused by that.

Eve chuckled. "She's more old school than anyone. Around here he goes by Ben, but officially he's Viscount Winford. It's one of his father's lesser titles, which he can use until he steps into his father's shoes. So he's referred to formally as Lord Winford."

I wondered suddenly if the family all wandered around inside that drafty manor house wearing their royal robes and calling each other by their titles. "Pass the salt, Your Ladyship. With pleasure, Lord Frome. Viscount Winford, will you have more gravy?"

Eve delivered the beer and returned. "Course, they're dying to get Ben married off. Lady Frome's shoved every debutante she can find under his nose. She's particularly interested in them if they have money as I hear the finances are a bit tight. Being the venue for *The Great British Baking Contest* was a godsend for the family."

I didn't care much about Lord Winford's future marriage to some rich blue blood to carry on his family dynasty. Right now, I was interested in my own family line. "It was strange, Eve. I felt almost as though Katie knew this Valerie but didn't want to talk about her. But I can't imagine why."

"You sound paranoid," she said, laughing gently. "Don't let the events of the weekend get to you. It was a long time ago. Maybe this Valerie simply wasn't memorable."

I thought of that vision I'd had. That distraught young

woman running away from Broomewode Hall, heavy with child, would have been memorable. Of that I was sure.

I'd been hustled out of that house like a common criminal. The Champneys were undoubtedly private people, but it felt like they were afraid to have a stranger ring their doorbell. Surely that wasn't normal behavior for people used to hosting grand dinners and balls.

I'd have continued chatting to Eve but behind her, Gerry appeared, head and shoulders only, between a bottle of gin and one of brandy. "I found my money," he told me in a hoarse whisper.

"Where?" I couldn't believe he'd found it.

"Where what, Poppy?" Eve asked me.

"Sorry, I was thinking aloud." I couldn't talk to Gerry like this. "I think I'll get some air. See you later."

I walked outside. There was a seating area for warmer weather, and by walking down a path I could settle my back against a tree and not be visible from the pub.

Gerry got right in my face, like a cool breeze. "My money is in Aaron Keel's car boot."

"If Aaron's got your winnings in the trunk of his car, then he must have killed you." I couldn't believe the electrician could take a loss at poker that hard. "Are you absolutely sure the money was yours?"

"Oh, yeah. He pulled into the parking area, and I watched him get out. I didn't like the look of him. Thought I'd have a search of his things, but he made it easy. Opened the boot to get something out and there was the stack of banknotes, half hidden under a box of light bulbs."

"He could have just been to the bank machine."

"Then why not stuff the cash in his wallet? No, Poppy. He stared at the money with a strange look on his face."

"Then what?" This was evidence. We had to tell the police.

"Then I came to find you. I'd have knocked him to the ground but that's difficult to do with no body."

"Okay. Let me think. We've got to somehow get the police to search Aaron's car." I couldn't tell them a ghost had told me where his stolen money was.

"That's him now," Gerry said. "He's gone into the bar."

I turned to follow and nearly bumped into Elspeth Peach. She looked as elegant as ever in a cream skirt suit and chocolate-colored scarf. It seemed that nothing could shake her unflappable demeanor. She looked serious and was carrying Gateau. The cat reached from Elspeth's arms and straight into mine. Gerry headed back into the bar and made waving motions for me to follow.

"There you are, dear Poppy. Is everything all right? Eve said you were acting strangely."

I didn't have time to explain. "I'm all right. There's so much going on here. Stranger and stranger things keep happening. I can't keep up."

"Don't worry. You've got people here looking out for you."

"Let's go for a walk and I'll explain." My plan was to head to the car park and take a look at Aaron's car for myself. Maybe Elspeth would have some idea how we could convince the police to search it. We'd barely gone ten steps when a shriek sounded out from the bar. It was Eve. I hoped Gerry hadn't decided to get all poltergeist on her. That seemed just the kind of prank he'd pull.

Elspeth ran to the sound and I followed.

"What happened?" Elspeth asked when she got to the bar. Eve shook her head, and her long braid flipped from side to side. "The tip jar is stacked full of cash. There must be hundreds of pounds in here. There's usually never more than a few quid."

I raced over to the bar, and sure enough, the silver beer tankard they used as a tip jar was bursting with cash. There was so much, notes were sticking out at odd angles. Even more alarming, Gerry was jumping up and down on top of the bar, face and fists screwed up, having a temper tantrum. "I watched him put the money in there when Eve's back was turned. I couldn't stop him. Now he'll get away with murder. My murder!"

"Where did he go?"

"Where did who go?" Eve was still staring at the tip jar.

Gaagh. I had to remember no one could see Gerry but me. "Aaron. I thought I saw him come in. Are the police finished with him?"

"I don't know, Poppy. I didn't see him. It's been so busy in here. All the locals coming in for a pint and a gossip."

Gerry jumped off the bar. "He went toward the guest rooms." He pointed to the door that led to our rooms. "I should have been a detective in my life rather than a reno guy." He twirled around. "If I had, I might still be alive."

Since I doubted he'd be any better behaved if he was on the police force, I kept my opinions to myself. Just as well, anyway, as I didn't want to appear to be talking to an imaginary friend.

"Could that be Gerry's missing money?" Elspeth asked, pointing to the money.

Gerry jumped onto the edge of the bar and swung his

legs, humming a football chant and looking pleased with himself. "Well done, Elspeth," he said. "Now work out that Aaron must have put it there."

"Are you okay, Poppy?" Eve asked. "You seem distracted. Kind of fidgety?"

I must have been swinging my head from side to side, watching Gerry's antics. "Sorry, I'm just thinking. Who's been through here who might have planted the money there?" *Aaron Keel. Say Aaron and then we can get the police.*

Eve looked puzzled. "Who would do that? Rob a dead man and then dump the cash for someone else to find?"

"The plot thickens," Gerry said.

I had to dig my nails into my hand to stop myself from telling him to shush.

"Perhaps someone is trying to cover their tracks and mislead everyone else," Elspeth said quietly. "I think the cash is a red herring and the money has nothing to do with Gerry's sad death." She shook her head. "This is such an awful business. I can't get over how something like this could happen on the show. We should have been protecting our contestants. They should have been safe under our care."

Eve leaned across the bar and rested her hand on Elspeth's. She told her not to be so hard on herself—no one could have predicted that such a terrible thing could happen here in sleepy Somerset. There was nothing anyone could have done.

"We need to report this to Sergeant Lane and DI Hembly," I said. Hopefully when they questioned her, Eve would remember that Aaron had walked through the pub only a few minutes before she found the money.

"Report what?" a voice asked. I turned, and in the

doorway to the bar stood Gordon. Eve explained what we'd found and how it looked like the winnings from the poker game. Gordon looked at the cash and then reached for the wad.

"Don't touch it!" I said sharply, but I was too late. He leafed through the money, surprised at the amount. "There's got to be four hundred quid here," he said. "That's a lot of cash to take off near strangers."

"Would somebody really kill another person because they lost at poker? It seems so extreme. But I guess it's up to the police to figure out," Eve added.

Gordon was still leafing through the cash in wonder. He whistled between his teeth.

"Shouldn't you stop touching the cash? The police might want to dust it for fingerprints," I said.

"I imagine there will be hundreds of fingerprints on these notes anyway. But the two cops are at the tent right now if you want to walk over. I was just up there to see if I could collect my toolbox, but it's all still sealed off. I'll come back with you, though. Could do with a bit of a leg stretch. And it's a gorgeous day out there."

He stuffed the cash back, approximately the way it had been. If the police found his fingerprints all over the notes, let him explain it.

I looked longingly at Elspeth, hoping she'd intervene and offer to walk with me instead. I wanted to tell her everything and get her advice. But Jonathon and Donald came in at that moment and said they wanted to meet. From their expressions, it was something serious, though I doubted it was more serious than me knowing who'd murdered Gerry and not being able to prove it.

"Maybe that's just a really generous tip," Gordon said. He leaned toward Eve. "That would buy you something nice."

"Much as I'd like that money," Eve said, "I'd like to put this whole weekend behind me more."

AFTER THE WARNING look I gave him, Gerry knew better than to follow me to the tent. I guessed he also didn't want to return to the site of his murder, either. He drifted off toward the guest rooms, no doubt to spy on Aaron. He saluted me as he left, as if we'd embarked on some kind of military mission.

Outside, the day had warmed and the sun was directly overhead. The scent of hyacinths sweetened the air. Gateau trotted happily by my side, more like a small guard dog than a cat. At least in all of this madness, I could count on Gateau to be my wing-cat.

Gordon squinted at the sun and pulled on a pair of dark sunglasses. He turned to me, smiling. "Glorious, isn't it? Nothing so nice as the English countryside when spring is in full swing." I nodded my agreement, wishing I could enjoy the spring day. Gordon was in good spirits, but I longed for some sense of normalcy again. I missed my quiet old cottage, the nights when Gina would come over with a bottle of wine and we'd cook a curry, chatting away while it bubbled on the stove. I thought about my parents in France, thinking I was having such a wonderful experience on the baking contest. I still wished I could call them, but they'd know immediately from my voice that something was wrong, and I didn't want to worry them.

"This murder is the most excitement we've had on the

Great British Baking Contest since that poor girl in season three slipped on half a pound of butter she'd dropped and sprained her ankle."

Maybe that's what had attracted everyone else to the show. Whether it was working behind the scenes or in front of the camera, everyone here seemed to be seduced by the drama. For my part, being filmed was unnerving. After watching the rushes, I'd seen how obviously nervous I was. Nothing about me said "natural performer." I preferred a quiet, anonymous life, creating beautiful graphics on my laptop at home, dealing with the clients on video calls from the comfort of my kitchen. I wouldn't have entered the contest in a million years if it hadn't been for that blanket. And now, here I was, embroiled in a murder case.

As if he'd been reading my mind, Gordon said, "I guess this wasn't what you were expecting when you came on the show, right?"

"Who could have predicted this? I can't stop thinking about the last time I saw Gerry, how convinced he was that someone was trying to sabotage him. I just thought he was being a sore loser and told him to drop the whole thing. But he was right. I feel like no one here is what they seem."

"Hey, you've got absolutely nothing to feel bad about, Poppy. Gerry *was* a sore loser. And personally, I feel bad for Marcus. What Gerry did was abominable. What could be worse than betrayal?" He grimaced and then seemed to gather himself, smiling brightly at me. "But I don't imagine a lovely young thing like you would have experienced that, though. Who could betray that gorgeous face?"

I blushed and shook my head. "Don't be silly, Gordon." Gateau mewed at my heels, and I bent to pick her up.

"I mean it, Poppy. You're a real beauty. There's something so wholesome about you. You're as sweet as American apple pie."

I frowned. Gordon was taking the compliments a little too far for a working relationship.

He must have misjudged why I felt uncomfortable. "I'm separated—about to get divorced. Don't tell me you haven't heard. I know how Gina gossips. Believe me, my marriage is over." He put his shoulders back. "I'm a free man now. Back on the market." He gave me a wink that reminded me a little of Gerry, but it felt awkward. Being in the tent surrounded by memories of death would be more comfortable than this conversation. I sped up my pace.

Thankfully, the tent was just ahead, and I escaped having to reply to Gordon as Sergeant Lane waved and walked toward us. I called out a hello, probably a little too enthusiastically.

The tent still looked strange without the bustling chaos of the cast and crew. A couple of uniformed officers were wandering the grounds, and red and white tape had made a mess of the manicured lawns. There were a few men and women in yellow neon jackets working the site.

"Poppy," Sergeant Lane said, smiling. "And your feline friend, I see. How are you today?"

"I'm all right. But Eve found a large sum of money stuffed into the tip jar. We believe it might be Gerry's winnings."

"Really?" Sergeant Lane said, scratching his head. "I'll come right away."

"The money wasn't there when she started her shift. See if she can remember who was in the pub who might have wanted to get rid of evidence." Gordon said the very thing I'd wanted to say.

The Sergeant looked at him oddly, maybe wondering why he was being given lessons in policing from the sound technician.

I'd have walked back up with Sergeant Lane, but Gina came running up to me. "Poppy!" I needed my best friend more than ever. I was so relieved to see her. There was so much to discuss, I didn't even know where to start. Each day here had been like a lifetime.

She seemed to feel the same. "Can we go for a walk?" she asked. "There's something I really need to talk to you about." She looked at Gordon apologetically. "It's girl stuff," she explained, shrugging.

"That's fine. I need to check my equipment, anyway. They told me to check with you to see if that's all right?" he asked Sergeant Lane, who said he could, so long as he didn't take anything away.

From the intense look on Gina's face, I felt a cold sensation of mounting trepidation spread across my body. I wasn't sure I could take any more bad news.

CHAPTER 15

*I*f I could describe Gina in three words, they would be: glossy, immaculate, and bubbly. So looking at her now, I could see that something was deeply wrong. She still looked perfectly turned out, and she'd done her hair in a French braid threaded through with black ribbon. However, rather than her usual toothy grin, she had a furrowed brow, and her eyes were full of concern. She took me by the hand, and we walked past the ornamental lake, the swans regal in their line formation, and the manicured garden beds that would soon be full of roses in bloom, until she turned in the direction of the forest and ushered me forward.

We headed for the footbridge I'd crossed only a few hours ago.

The sun broke through the leafy canopy, casting angled shadows on the forest floor, and I could smell the beautiful bluebells before we even stepped foot into the shade. I noticed that Gateau had wandered off again. That cat was either all over me or nowhere to be seen. I trusted what Elspeth said, though, that Gateau and I had chosen each other. My feline friend always seemed to return to me the moment I needed her most.

Gina hadn't spoken a single word for the duration of the walk, and to say I was worried was an understatement. Normally I couldn't stop her from incessant chatting. It was one of the things that made her such a great hair and makeup artist: She knew exactly how to put people at ease. Finally she stopped, and letting my hand drop, she turned to face me. We'd been going so fast, we were both a little out of breath.

"Goodness, Gina, what is it? You're terrifying me!" The sun had gone behind the trees, and I pulled my linen shirt tight around my body. The fabric was too flimsy to be protective or warm.

She took a few deep breaths and gathered herself before letting her words tumble out. "I went to the tent this morning to pack up my makeup bags and hair tools, and before they realized I was standing there, I overheard the policemen talking. They said it was almost certain that someone in the cast or the crew of the show murdered Gerry. It was no accident. They've ruled out the possibility of any strangers being able to access the set that day."

She stopped and took another deep breath. "Poppy, that means it's one of us! You cannot trust *anyone* you've met here. No one. Right now, some crazy murderer is running around, and even the people who seem super kind and lovely are potential threats. You need to stay away from *everyone* you've met here until this is sorted."

She put her hands on her hips, her signature move for when she meant business. I tried to tell her that I was grateful she was being protective, but I'd only really made friends with Gerry, Florence, and Elspeth from the show. One was dead, the other was too concerned about her nail polish to have time to think about murdering anybody, and Elspeth Peach was a national treasure and the same age as Gina's grandmother—surely she couldn't be warning me to stay away from her.

"I know. You've missed a lot of it, but we've all come to realize it was someone we know." I caught my lower lip between my teeth. Should I tell her about Aaron? No. Better to wait until the police worked out who'd done it.

"But you were with Gordon just now. I don't think we can trust him. I know all of the crew so much better than you, Poppy, and Gordon has had some serious issues of his own."

I asked her to explain what she meant. Gina was always happy to gossip. "Gordon used to be one of the most happy-go-lucky guys on the crew. He was known as a bit of a jack-the-lad, always pulling silly pranks like putting a Whoopi cushion on Elspeth's seat or planting fake spiders in the sandwiches. Used any opportunity to tell a silly joke. He was a lovable goof and popular on set. But midway through the last season, when Gordon turned up to work one morning, it was like he was a different person. Gone were the jokes and pranks, and in their place was a moody, irritable, and irrational man."

"Really? He seems so friendly."

"He's better now, but back then he barely spoke, and when he did it was to snap at people over nothing. It was like he'd had a personality transplant. It was really affecting morale, so the crew staged an intervention. Gordon broke down and said that after working with the baking show for so long, he and his wife had wanted a better kitchen. They hired a contractor for a full kitchen renovation. They wanted to fully gut it and build their dream one from scratch. You know the kind of thing: floating island, swing-door cabinets, marble work surfaces, granite tiles on the floor. The lot. It took ages."

"That's stressful on anyone." I remembered when my parents renovated our Seattle kitchen. It was tough on all of us.

"But when the renovation was almost complete, Gordon came home from work early one day and found his wife in bed with the contractor. He was devastated and handled it badly. He threw his wife out, attacked the contractor and tried to smash up the new kitchen, but it had been so well built, he could barely mark it.

"We all felt terrible for him and did everything we could to make him feel better. Took turns having him over for dinner, nights out at the pub. We even organized a couple of fun staff trips to paintball and abseiling. But nothing worked. That is, until the season ended. In the break, he went on a cruise by himself to see the Northern Lights and came back a changed man. He was jolly and outgoing again. Couldn't speak highly enough about traveling and seeing things abroad. The cruise seemed to have done the trick."

"I'd say it did. He was just hitting on me."

She leaned forward. "Don't date him, Pops. I'm telling you, he's got a bad temper."

"Don't worry. I'd never date Gordon Bennett. He gave me the creeps."

"I just can't help worrying about the similarities between what happened to him and what happened to Marcus." She shook her head. "But there are thousands of contractors.

And how could Gerry possibly be the man he'd found in bed with his wife? One of them would have said something."

It was twisted logic, and it took me a moment to catch up. "Oh, Gina. You don't think Gerry slept with Gordon's wife, do you?"

"I don't know," she said, shaking her head. "Wouldn't it be too much of a coincidence that he made off with Marcus's *and* Gordon's wife? Gerry's not that hot."

I was glad Gerry had stayed at the inn—he'd surely take great offense at that. "And if it wasn't Gerry who slept with Gordon's wife, then he'd have no reason to kill the man."

I couldn't tell her that Aaron Keel was the prime suspect, at least on my list, not without explaining that I'd received a hot tip from a ghost. Anyway, Gordon had mentioned the money timeline to Sergeant Lane, so hopefully they'd track the cash back to Aaron within a few hours and this would all be over.

But wait. Gordon had only walked in after Eve had found the money. I'd been standing there the whole time he was flipping through the cash and then we'd left the pub together. Eve had never said anything about the money not being there when she started her shift.

I was thinking furiously. Could Gordon have planted the money on Aaron? Could the over-friendly sound guy have killed Gerry? "What if he wanted to rid the world of all contractors who seduce their clients?" I was stretching here, but Elspeth had told me to follow my intuition, and it was definitely pulling me along this path.

Gina shook her head. "But how would he even know that Gerry had seduced Marcus's wife? It's not like they were friends, and if Gerry had boasted over a poker game, Gordon wasn't there to hear it. So I'm imagining things."

She made to turn back, but I stopped her. "Gordon did know about Gerry and Marcus's wife," I told her. "He heard him admit to the affair."

Her eyes went round. "What?"

"We were mic'd. I remember Gordon warned us that anything we said would be overheard. It was when Marcus first acted rude to Gerry. I honestly don't think he'd noticed him, and then after Marcus was rude to him, he suddenly laughed and said he'd renovated Marcus's house. He even joked that Marcus's wife was hot and if he had spent time with her, he'd added those hours to his bill."

"Gordon is almost as good an electrician as Aaron is. Pops, we have to tell the police." I shivered. Gordon had been flirting with me only minutes before.

There was a crunch of branches breaking underfoot, and I felt a sudden spear of terror. "I don't think that's a very good idea," said Gordon.

Gina and I froze. I reached out and took her hand so that we stood facing him, united. I couldn't believe he'd followed us into the forest without us noticing. He must have been deadly quiet, or, more likely, we'd been so engaged in our conversation that we hadn't paid attention to noises around us.

"Girls, girls," he said. "Why do you look scared? Come on, it's me. The weekend has gotten to you both. I'm not the monster you think I am. You need to calm down."

Gina glanced at me and back at him. "We were talking about family. Not about you, Gordon." She laughed. "Don't go getting paranoid."

He made a tsking sound and came closer. He held out something small and black. "This is a directional microphone. I rarely use it, but it's very good for picking up conversations outside of normal hearing range. Still think I'm being paranoid?"

I put my free hand on my amethyst. I hoped Elspeth had put a doozy of a protection spell on this stone because I had a feeling I was going to need it. I cringed, realizing I'd called Gordon creepy and he'd heard me.

"No one thinks you're a monster," Gina said, her voice trembling a little. "We were just worried about you. You've had a rough year."

"That little story you just spun to darling Poppy here didn't sound like concern. It sounded more like fear-mongering. And slander."

"Absolutely. You could sue us," I said. Let him get a lawyer, anything, but please let us get out of here.

He took a step forward. I flinched. My heart was pounding against my amethyst, and I could hear blood rushing in my ears. Sweat began to gather at the bottom of my back.

"Come on, Poppy. Don't look so afraid. It's just Gordy here, your lovable sound guy. I only followed you to invite you for a drink tonight."

He'd heard us figure out he'd probably killed Gerry, was he playing some sick game of cat and mouse?

"Poppy doesn't want to go for a drink with you. I think you should let us pass," Gina said. I felt her hand shaking, and I gripped it tighter. Above our heads, the birds were flying between the trees, rustling the leaves and chirping to one another. The scent of bluebells was suddenly sickly sweet, too pungent, too cloying.

"I think Poppy can answer for herself," Gordon said, gritting his teeth.

I tried to smile brightly, anything to show Gordon that I wasn't going to be bulldozed by his psychopathic mind games. "Gina's right. I'm not really in the mood for a night at the pub."

"You want to run to the police and tell them a bunch of lies. It wasn't Gerry who renovated my kitchen."

"Of course, it wasn't," I said.

"Do you think I'd have worked with the man who seduced my wife? Don't be crazy."

Despite his attempt at being convincing, I still didn't believe a word he was saying. His smile was unnatural and there was a sheen to his skin that I didn't like. My eyes darted about the forest, looking for the best exit, and then I sized Gordon up. He was a little paunchy around the belly. I figured we had a chance to outrun him, especially if we headed in opposite directions. I looked down, hoping he couldn't see my lips, and whispered, "You run for the tent, I'll head for the pub." One of us ought to be able to reach help.

"Why are you planning an escape route, Poppy? I just told you there's nothing to worry about." He shook his head. "I'd have liked to take you out for a nice dinner tonight."

"Look, you were under stress. Everyone will understand," Gina said.

He sighed. "You're a lovely young woman, Gina. So is Poppy. But the two of you have some serious trust issues. I overheard you telling Poppy about my cruise, but you missed the best part. I went to see the Northern Lights and it was beneath those mesmerizing lights, the swirls of emerald green and vivid pink and intense blues, beneath that absolute wonder of the universe that I decided. I wouldn't let anyone ever get away with infidelity again. I vowed to become vigilant, to keep my eyes and ears open for any would-be cheaters, any men who thought that a woman's marriage vows weren't worth the paper they were written on. So imagine my joy when the show brought one such specimen right to me. You were all warned, weren't you, not to discuss private matters while your mics were on? But I guess Gerry thought he was above that, just as he did when he slept with Marcus's wife."

He'd been talking with rapid speed, eager to spill his story. He stopped and caught his breath. He was smiling again, and it was not an endearing smile.

"I heard Gerry telling you he was going to have another look at his oven. I had no idea I wasn't the only one with a vendetta against Gerry and that Marcus was actually sabotaging Gerry—he really helped me out. I'll have to buy him a drink sometime. Even Aaron did me a favor, making threats over that poker game.

"After everyone left, I took jumper cables from the boot of my car, attached one end to the electrical supply and the other side to a leg at the back. It was pretty ingenious, if I say so myself. When Gerry returned to the tent to examine the oven, as I knew he would, I turned the power on, and he was electrocuted the second he touched the oven handle."

My eyes widened in horror. I couldn't believe I'd ever been nice to this guy.

"When Marcus managed to convince the police he wasn't the culprit, I planted the poker winnings in Aaron's car. Bad luck that he found them before the police. Still, I'm sure they'll get around to him. He is the obvious suspect."

I was calling Elspeth and Gateau in my mind, but I was so scared I doubted the message was getting through.

"You have to admire my plan," Gordon continued. "No one suspected me until you."

"Run!" I cried to Gina. We broke into a run in separate directions. He couldn't follow both of us, so hopefully one of us would get to help. The soil was wet underfoot, and my trainers sank into its depths. My head was whirring. There were broken branches and twigs everywhere. I mustn't fall like poor Katie Donegal and break a bone.

All those months of practice baking, and I'd let my exercise regime go to the dogs. How I wished I'd kept up my track training. But I didn't get very far before I heard a piercing scream from Gina. I stopped dead and spun on my heels. I couldn't go for help and leave Gina, not if he was hurting the closest thing I had to a sister.

Gina was on the ground, and Gordon was tackling her. I ran straight toward them, faster than I'd ever run in my whole life, no longer concerned about the mud and twigs. I just wanted to get that beast off of her. I was only a meter away when I saw the knife. The handle was burnished black, and the silver blade was long and gleaming. I froze.

Elspeth said I was a witch. She said I had powers. If that was true, I really needed them now. I raised my voice. "Sisters, mothers, fellow witches, please help me stop this monster in his tracks. Dull his knife and his senses." Then I added the witches' blessing, "Blessed be."

It was no kind of a spell, but I was untried, untrained and it was all I had. Gordon didn't immediately turn into a frog, the knife didn't fly out of his hand, but I felt an immense power surging through my body.

Still, I couldn't reach her before he could hurt her. Fury, fear, love, it condensed like a ball of fire. I had no idea where it was coming from, but it took over like a life force. My hands filled with a jolt of electricity, a force I'd never felt before, and as I turned my open palms toward Gordon, I yelled, "Get off her!"

A beam of light seemed to fly from my hands and hit him in the back. He flew off of Gina's body, into the air, and then slumped back against a tree stump.

Amazed, I bent down to Gina and pulled her to her feet.

"What on earth?" she began to say, staring wide-eyed at me.

Gordon was moaning in pain, but I saw that he was already reaching for the fallen blade. I grabbed for the knife while Gina yelled for help. Our cries echoed around the forest. I lunged, slipping in the mud as he was reaching. His fingers were on the knife handle.

"I don't think so, Gordon," said a familiar voice.

Elspeth! And by her feet was Gateau. Elspeth raised her arms, the wide sleeves of her billowy silk shirt catching the breeze, and began to say something in what sounded like Latin. The air became suddenly very still. Elspeth's face was fierce in its concentration.

Gordon's hands dropped to his sides, and he rolled back onto the ground. "What's happening to me?" he murmured. "What's happening?" He gripped his knees and moaned in confusion.

I stood back from Gordon. "Elspeth, you came."

"I told you, Poppy. You're not alone anymore. My dear girl,

you and I have a lot to talk about, but right now, the most pressing matter is tying this scoundrel up. At the moment, he's too weak to move, but I can only hold him so long. You need to find something to tie him with."

I rushed to Elspeth's bag (a red Hermes Birkin bag, I couldn't help but notice—she really was a classy lady), but inside was only a tube of Chanel lipstick, a wallet, a big leather-bound book, and a huge set of keys. Apart from hitting him over the head with the book, nothing in there was helpful. I looked back at Elspeth, who was frowning in concentration, hands still out in front of her. Her scarf!

I slipped her silk scarf from around her neck and tied Gordon's hands behind him. His eyes were wild, but his limbs were slack. I had no idea how to tie people up, so I tied as many tight knots as I could. "Gina, you and I can sit on Gordon until Elspeth can find help."

Gina, dazed from the tackle and Elspeth's sudden appearance, finally came to and said, "Poppy, the ribbon in my hair. It's long, and we might be able to secure his feet with that." She tugged at the black satin ribbon that was threaded into her French plait. It must have been about a meter long. She really did know how to be inventive with hair! Gina quickly unbraided her braid and released the ribbon.

I rolled him onto his belly and made that guy eat dirt. Gina joined me, and we both sat on his back as she wound the ribbon around his ankles twice over and then tied an expert knot. Gordon spluttered and coughed out some soil. Turning his head to the side, he spat and said, "You're making a very big mistake, ladies," he said. "No one will believe you. It's your word against mine, and the police don't have a thing on me."

"We'll leave that for them to decide, shall we?" Elspeth said, grimacing in concentration. She finally let her hands return to her sides and stood taking deep breaths. "Gina and Poppy, do you think you can hold him down until I come back? I'll rush over to the tent and tell Detective Inspector Hembly we've apprehended the culprit and could use a little backup."

But I could feel Gordon's legs struggling and bucking against the ribbon. "Elspeth, I don't think the ribbon will hold. It's already starting to come loose," I said.

"His belt!" Gina cried out. "Can you keep him weak for one more minute? I can slide off his belt, and we can use that for his feet."

Poor Elspeth was clearly exhausted. Whatever it was she was doing really was taking its toll. Her calm and composed face was strained with effort, and the color seemed to be draining out of it with each second passing. She raised her hands again, and I saw a bead of sweat gather at her temple. We both jumped off Gordon's back, rolled him over, and Gina worked with her super-fast hairdresser hands to loosen his belt. Gordon kept muttering, "get off me, get off me" over and over, but he was so confused by what was happening, his protests were barely audible. Gina took the belt and cinched his ankles together. We pushed him back down and resumed our positions.

Elspeth let her hands drop again. "I'll be as quick as I can."

There was a crunch of twigs underfoot, and a familiar voice said, "I heard screaming." It was Sergeant Lane. He caught his breath and stared at us. "What's been going on here?"

We must have looked a strange bunch, both of us sitting on Gordon, who was tied up with a Hermes scarf, a hair ribbon and a belt.

"They attacked me," Gordon sputtered. "Get them off. I want them charged with assault."

The sergeant came toward us. Whatever Elspeth had done, it was wearing off, and it was getting harder and harder to keep our prisoner still. I dug my knee into the small of his back, and he yelped in pain.

"He's confessed to Gerry's murder, and he tried to stab me," Gina cried. "The knife is there." She pointed at the wicked blade on the ground.

Behind the sergeant, a uniformed constable came running. At Lane's order, he took a pair of silver handcuffs from the side of his trousers. We jumped off Gordon's back, and while the constable handcuffed him, the sergeant formally arrested him and read him his rights. Gordon stopped struggling and lay very still, deadly still, as if this were all a dream and any moment he could wake up.

Sergeant Lane pulled Gordon to his feet and held out Elspeth's scarf for her to take. He looked as though he might say something, then just shook his head.

The two men escorted their prisoner back, and we three women followed. Sergeant Lane told DI Hembly what had happened, and they walked Gordon over to their police car. It was like watching a TV cop drama, the steps surrounding the arrest were so familiar, but I'd signed up for a baking show, not this. The blue lights flicked on and they put Gordon in the back, then the car sped away from us.

The faster, the better.

CHAPTER 16

*G*ina and I clutched hot mugs of steaming tea while Elspeth dished out clotted cream fudge. We were both still shaking. I'd known Gina all my life, and I'd never seen her so lost for words. She kept opening her mouth to speak and then closing it again. Her lovely long hair was crinkled from the braid, and it hung in waves over her shoulders. Somehow, during all the excitement, she managed to stay looking pretty.

The noise had alerted the others at the inn, and by the time the three of us walked back, we had an audience. Several humans and one ghost, who gave me a huge grin and two thumbs up.

When she saw the state Gina and I were in, Eve made us hot drinks, her hands trembling a little as we told her about Gordon and our time in the forest. We'd have to give statements down at the police station later, but for now we had some time to recoup and process the craziness that had just happened.

Elspeth came to join us, clutching a hot mug of creamy-looking cocoa and the box of fudge. She'd tied her neckerchief around the straps of her bag, and now I could see her throat, the pale and delicate skin and the pattern of her blue veins. It was easy to forget that Elspeth was Gina's grandmother's age. She was so elegant and composed, and her slim frame added to the sprightly and youthful air she showed on the screen. But now she looked worn out. No doubt we did, too.

"I don't understand how you got Gordon off me," Gina said. "I saw the knife. I was certain he was going to..." She couldn't finish the sentence.

I glanced at Elspeth, who gave a tiny shake of her head. No mention of witches. I went with what I thought was part of the truth. "When someone you love is in trouble, you find extra strength."

"That's true," Hamish said, sipping a whiskey. "I once witnessed a mother lift a car off her child when it was pinned underneath. Most extraordinary what we can do to save those we love."

She leaned over and gripped my hand. "Thanks, Pops."

Marcus was drinking a fancy coffee, as he was heading back to London soon. He looked pretty relieved to see someone else charged with Gerry's murder. "So Gordon killed Gerry to punish him for sleeping with *my* wife?"

"I think it became an obsession with him," I said. "He couldn't kill the man who'd seduced his wife without being the obvious suspect, so he decided to kill other seducers. When he overheard Gerry telling me the story of your renovation and how he'd had an affair with your wife, he decided to punish him by proxy, I suppose."

"And I was nearly charged with the murder," Marcus grumbled.

"You didn't come off as badly as me, mate," Gerry complained from his perch on the window ledge.

"Aaron was the other likely suspect," Elspeth said. "He was the electrician, after all, and he'd lost all that money to Gerry. It did seem like his crime, which meant Gordon nearly got away with it."

"But why did Gordon put the poker winnings in my tip jar?" Eve asked. She was sitting down for once, enjoying a drink herself.

Aaron was sitting near the back and he looked at his feet. "Aaron?" I prompted. "Do you want to explain?"

He glared at me, but nodded. "I found the money in the boot of my car. I knew someone had planted it on me. Since I'd already endured a very unpleasant interview with the police, I decided to get rid of the money."

Elspeth tsked at him, looking disappointed. "If you'd gone to the police, they might have caught Gordon sooner and Poppy and Gina wouldn't have been nearly killed."

"Sorry," he mumbled. "But I thought I was in for it. Him being electrocuted and me being pretty free with the threats."

"Yes. You really played into Gordon's hands, there," Jonathon said. His tone was hard.

"Gordon's almost as good an electrician as I am," Aaron reminded us.

Hamish nodded. "Once Gerry had been electrocuted, Gordon turned the power off at the breaker and removed the cables. He put them back in his car. Now forensics have hold of them, they can likely prove that those cables were used in the murder. He'd made sure that it was only the breaker for

Gerry's oven that was live, and that's why none of the others showed any signs of being messed with. It was surprisingly clever. And Gordon might have gotten away with it, if it wasn't for you two. He couldn't resist boasting about how he'd executed the whole thing."

"He was planning to kill us, so he could boast all he liked," Gina said. "Isn't that just like a man?"

"Come now, that's not very fair," Donald said as he came back into the bar. Now that someone had been arrested, Donald had returned to his smooth, showbizzy self. Gone were the frown lines that had been etched into his forehead, and there was a flush of pink to his previously pallid cheeks. His linen suit was ironed and only creased at the knees, and his hair had been swept away from his face again. It was like he'd pressed a reset button. "Not all men are the same," he insisted. "Look at some of the contestants here, for example. Isn't Hamish lovely, and Gaurav, Ewan and Daniel too. It's easy to focus on the bad eggs, but we have so many splendid people on the show."

He went on to enthuse about how this tragedy had brought us bakers closer together. As we healed our wounds, we'd become closer as a cast. It was a touching idea, but I was finding it hard to wrap my head around the prospect of baking again. How was I going to recoup my energies and concentrate on chocolate tortes and making madeleines?

"The next ordeal will be giving my statement to the police. I'll have to relive it all again." Gina looked terrified. I reached out and took her hand to squeeze it. "You'll be fine. All you have to do is tell the truth. And you're the queen of that. I always come to you when I need someone to dish it like it is."

She gave a little laugh and stood to leave, stretching out her back like a cat. "I'd better do something about my hair before I go anywhere."

Elspeth looked at me. "I think you and I could benefit from a walk. Some fresh air and a chat?"

I agreed, and after Donald telling us not to venture too far from the inn, Elspeth linked my arm, and we set out.

As we walked, the pebbled path crunched beneath our shoes. Elspeth bent down and picked a daisy from the lawn. She twirled it between her slender fingers and seemed to be deep in private thoughts. It was hard to imagine that just over an hour ago, I'd been sitting on the back of a murderer, trying to stop him from stabbing my best friend. I shivered. I must have looked wiped and also perplexed because Elspeth said, "My dear child, you've had the most extraordinary forty-eight hours, and I'm guessing that you have many questions for me."

"Elspeth, I don't even know where to begin."

She kept walking, and my feet followed her of their own accord. My thoughts were crashing about like a stormy sea. She looked into the distance where Broomewode Hall stood at the top of the hill and said gently, "Poppy, you have some extraordinary gifts, the full extent of which I don't think you yet realize."

"I called for help. I was so desperate when Gina was in danger. I made something up and called for my sisters and mothers. I don't even remember what I said. But some force did come over me. And then you arrived."

"Yes. I told you, you're not alone. And, of course, I was particularly sensitive to you, as I'd made you that protection spell."

"The stone was like a homing device?" I touched the amethyst I still wore.

She laughed softly. "Something like that."

We turned away from Broomewode Hall and the vast white tent, whose calico awnings had witnessed both the highest joys and deepest horrors over the past few days. The forest was ahead of us, and we both turned instinctively away from there, too, and instead toward a rose garden that was not yet in bloom. I stared at the almost empty flowerbeds, the long necks of the bushes that would be weighed down with heavy petals within the next couple of months. And then I told the great Elspeth Peach some things about my life that only Gina and my parents knew. I visualized a soft yellow rose blooming, and I opened up in a way that I had never done before with a stranger.

I began with how I'd arrived at the Philpotts' bakery and no one had ever been able to find my mother. I explained to Elspeth about some of the ghosts I'd seen. I found spirits to be good company and, on the whole, a friendly and even informative bunch. I told her that I'd seen Gerry today, and that he'd helped solve his own murder. I shared how Mildred, the ghost who dwelled in my cottage's kitchen, had previously been a cook, and she'd helped me practice for the baking contest. It was wonderful to talk about all the things I usually kept secret.

I even admitted that really I'd come on the show for one reason only: to try and find out more about my birth parents. I'd spotted the same pattern as my blanket in an oil painting hanging in Broomewode Hall. That's why I was really here.

I paused and took another deep breath. I could feel the

warm rays of the sun on my neck. I couldn't believe all of this had just poured out of me.

"It must be very hard not to know where you came from," she said. "But I think I might be able to throw a little light on the origins of your special gift."

We had finished circling the rose garden, and Elspeth led me to a bench on the path. "We witches are blessed with incredible gifts of healing, intuition, and we can cast spells that disrupt the natural order of things, for good or bad. That is down to the individual witch, but I already know that you are one of the good ones."

"But I've never done anything except see ghosts." I remembered the power surge when I'd thrown Gordon against the tree. "Until today."

"Oh, you've got the power. It's simply been dormant. You had no one to teach you. Your ability to see spirits, however, was too strong to be suppressed. It is a great privilege and an honor to be a witch, Poppy. You will have come from a great line of witches in your family. It is passed down through the maternal side. No wonder you feel such a strong urge to try and find your mother."

Elspeth stopped talking and put her hand to my cheek. A great warmth spread throughout my body, and my heartbeat began to regulate. Gradually I felt calm and soothed. I took long, slow breaths. My lungs expanded and contracted, expanded and contracted. The rhythm was pleasant, and in fact, I felt more at peace than I had in a long time.

"Feel better?" she asked, taking her hand away and resting it on the bench.

I nodded.

"Witches have great empathy, Poppy. I can see that in you.

You're trying to understand the world and your own place within it. You have an open heart and an open mind."

I nodded again. I had no idea what to say.

"It's no coincidence that you found yourself here at Broomewode Hall," Elspeth continued. "In addition to the blanket you saw in the painting, the manor house has pulled you towards it in other, even more mysterious ways. You see, Broomewode Hall is an energy vortex that draws witches to it as it expands their sensitivity and power. Your natural witchy powers that you were born with will have been strengthening and developing since you arrived. This is a good place for you to begin to learn your craft."

It was all beginning to make sense, but then I remembered that Jonathon had been talking to Gateau, how they seemed to be communicating with each other. What could that have been about? Were my powers already misbehaving? I explained to Elspeth what I'd felt and seen, but again, she didn't seem surprised.

"Men can be witches, too, you know. It isn't just women. Nursery rhymes and fairy tales have filled young minds with nonsense. It makes me quite furious. Our Jonathon is also a witch, a somewhat naughty one, in fact, but perhaps that is a story for another time. There is one more thing that you must take on board: When I told you that you and Gateau had found one another, I wasn't exaggerating. She is your familiar, Poppy. You must respect her and look after her, because she is there to keep you safe from harm."

Ah, my sweet little Gateau. Just the thought of her calmed me down.

"You must have more questions for me, but I think perhaps that is enough for today. We have plenty of time to get to know one another better, and I will guide you through this new development in your life. You won't be alone."

I had a sudden awful thought. "But what if I'm voted off next week, Elspeth? I'm not as good a baker as Maggie or Florence. I couldn't bear it if I had to go home. Is there a way to magic me into remaining on the show so that I can stay closer to Broomewode Hall?"

Elspeth's faced suddenly changed, and she became instantly serious. "No, no, Poppy. You cannot ever ever *ever* use your powers for personal gain. It goes against the greatest and most important law of witchhood. You'll just have to keep practicing your baking like everyone else."

I felt like pouting. What was the point of being a witch if I couldn't even use a spell to keep me on a baking show?

"You must work extra hard this week. Practice, practice, practice. And next week, put your best fondant forward, so to speak."

"And how will I learn all the stuff I should have before now? All the witchy things?"

She laughed. "That, also, involves practice. You've a long road ahead of you, Poppy, but I suspect it will be an exciting one."

CHAPTER 17

*J*f I had begun the weekend thinking that my biggest life-changing moment was getting the call that I'd been chosen to compete in *The Great British Baking Contest,* it was only because I had no idea what was coming. I'd always known that the origins of my birth made me a little different than my friends. Unlike Gina, I didn't have any red-faced screaming baby photos of me in the hospital or touching ones where I was asleep on my mom's chest. There was never evidence of those very first moments when life comes hurtling into the world and is greeted by those who made it. In that sense, something had always been missing, and I'd grown up desperate to know more about my origins.

Finally, I understood. There was a whole other dimension to my being that I had no idea about. I was a witch.

Elspeth pointed over to the manor house. The sun had moved across the sky, and now the top of the golden stone looked as if a halo of light shone around it. "Beautiful, isn't it?" she said.

Last year, at home in my cottage watching *The Great*

British Baking Contest, I had begun my quest to find out more about Broomewode Hall. But now that I was finally here, when I thought I was actually going to get some answers, it was even more of a mystery to me. Not in my wildest dreams would I have imagined that beyond the intrigue of the blanket in the oil painting, there was something deeper, something more integral to my being, something more...*magical* about the place that had drawn me to it. I thought I was getting closer to understanding where I'd come from, but in reality, I was starting this journey from scratch. It reminded me of all that practice pastry-making Mildred had made me do at home. She made me throw away countless wads of dough she deemed too sticky or too dry and forced me to start again from the beginning. But in the end, I was thankful for Mildred; she taught me how to persevere and not accept anything less than perfect. I knew that in the weeks to come, I was going to have to rely on this tenacity— both when baking and learning more about who I really was.

To think that just a couple of days ago, my biggest worry had been baking in front of cameras and freaking out about how the world at home would be watching my every move. Now, I couldn't believe how nervous I was about something so simple. In the time since, I'd had to deal with finding a dead body, apprehending a murderer, and discovering I was a witch. If only I'd known how good I had it before, maybe I would have performed on the show with a little more confidence and pizzazz, rather than cowering at the cameras.

We stood from the bench, and as if she'd been summoned, Gateau trotted over to us.

"There you are, my gorgeous kitty," I cooed. The three of us walked back to the inn.

Maggie, Hamish and Florence were in the entranceway as we walked in.

Florence ran over and nearly sent me flying to the floor with an enormous bear hug. "My goodness, Poppy!" she cried at me. "What did I tell you about keeping safe? Only this morning I was telling you off for going out walking, and then you do it again and nearly get yourself killed! I could kill you myself for being so reckless, except I'm so happy you're okay!" She released me from her grip and looked into my eyes for an awkwardly long time. "You seem, I don't know, kind of different. It's weird. You look more at peace somehow? How is that possible when some psycho killer tried to attack you?"

I laughed and told her off for being dramatic. But she had hit the nail on the head; I did feel oddly calmer. Perhaps it was Elspeth's magic, or maybe just knowing that Gerry's killer had been caught had set my busy mind to rest. Maggie and Hamish came to embrace me, and we stood like that for a moment, in a group hug. At least I now knew I could trust them.

"Everyone is finally allowed to leave," Maggie said.

"Our little world is back to normal now," Elspeth replied. Hah, she could speak for herself on that one. "We can put all the horribleness of this weekend behind us and look forward to some excellent baking in the next few weeks," she continued. "Don't forget, practice makes perfect."

We all hugged again, and Florence, Maggie, and Hamish lugged their suitcases to their respective cars. I waved them off, sad to see them go but happy we'd all be back next weekend, hopefully with all that drama as ancient history.

I turned to Elspeth. She smiled generously, showing off her set of perfectly straight white teeth. "I'm due at the police station, Poppy. And then it's your turn. We'll talk some more soon, but for now I think you have enough to comprehend." She pressed her business card into my hand. It was made of thick, smooth manila paper, *Elspeth Peach, Author & Master Baker* embossed in glinting gold foil. She tapped the phone number at the bottom and said, "Call me anytime. No witch is ever alone. I know it wasn't quite the family you were looking for, but we are a family nonetheless."

"I thought I'd been given a clue when an old woman here called me Valerie and suggested she used to work at Broomewode Hall in the kitchen. On my way up, I had a vision of a woman running from the hall. She was heavily pregnant. Elspeth, I think it was my mother, but no one at the Hall seems to remember her. Or they pretend they don't." I was so frustrated, and I was sure it came out in my tone.

"Always so impatient," she chided. "I believe I told you that now you've got another family. Remember, child, if you're a witch, your mother was most likely one too. Someone in the coven will remember her."

And just like that, my hope was back. Elspeth was right. Broomewode Hall might refuse to give me answers, but somewhere, somehow, I'd find out what had happened to my mother.

I hugged her goodbye and climbed the stairs to my bedroom. Inside, Gerry was waiting for me.

"That's nice, isn't it!" he said as I walked into the room. "Gordon killed me. I never did anything to him. I'd no idea he was so unhinged."

"Oh, Gerry, I'm so sorry. But I'm glad he's been caught. He'll go to jail for a very long time. And now you can move on."

"I don't think I'll be doing that," he said. "It was too much fun playing detective. I wasn't messing when I said that's what I should have done instead of renovations. I think I'll be sticking around for a while longer, in case my skills are needed. Plus, look what I've just learned to do."

He hopped down from the chest of drawers, headed for the door and floated right through it!

"See you next week, Poppy," he called out.

I turned, laughing, and started to throw my clothes into my weekend bag.

DOWNSTAIRS, the inn was eerily quiet. I took my bag to my car, and as I opened the door, I heard an angry meow. And then another. I looked down, and Gateau was waiting for me. "I'm so sorry, my little puss. Don't think I forgot about you. The passenger seat is ready and waiting." I held the door for her as if she were the Queen of England and laughed as she eyed the jump to the seat, took a few steps back and then leapt right in. I shut the door and got in the other side, leaning over to stroke Gateau's soft head and touch her little nose with mine.

As I turned my key in the ignition, I took one last look at Broomewode Hall in the distance. I made a silent vow that next week, no matter what happened, I would find out the true identity of Valerie. Was she a real person, or was Valerie just the fantasy of a sweet old lady suffering with dementia? I guessed that on top of searching for my family, I'd also have to get to grips with my new powers. I wondered what exactly I could do—there must be a way for my powers to help me with my quest, but Elspeth's warning rang heavy in my ears. I couldn't use my powers for gain, whatever they might be. And if that wasn't enough stress to contend with for one week, I only had five days until I had to return to the competition tent.

A Note from Nancy

Dear Reader,

Thank you for reading The Great Witches Baking Show. I have plenty more stories about Poppy, Elspeth and friends planned for the future.

I hope you'll consider leaving a review and please tell your friends who like cozy mysteries and culinary adventures.

Review on Amazon, Goodreads or BookBub.

I love you more than apple pie! And speaking of pies— turn the page for Poppy's recipe for Tarte au Citron.

Join my newsletter at nancywarren.net for unique content no one else receives.

Until next time,

Nancy

POPPY'S RECIPE FOR TARTE AU CITRON

Florence's tarte au citron may have won first place in the afternoon's competition, but it wasn't because her recipe was any better than mine! Below find my ingredients list and method for—as Jonathon so inelegantly called it—the perfect marriage of zing and cream! This recipe serves eight people, or, if your appetite is more like mine, then a hungry six. If you're short of time on the day, you can make this tart up to two days ahead of serving. And if, for some crazy reason, you end up with leftovers, it also freezes well.

Ingredients:

Pastry

- 175g/6oz plain flour
- 100g/4oz cold butter, cut into small cubes
- 25g/1oz icing sugar
- 1 large egg, beaten
- 2 tbsp water

Lemon Filling

- 5 large eggs
- 125ml/4 fl oz double cream
- 225g/8oz caster (superfine) sugar
- finely grated zest and juice of 4 large lemons

Method:

1. First up, rummage through your cupboards and find a 23cm/9-inch deep loose-bottomed tart tin.
2. To make the pastry, measure the flour, butter and sugar and add them all directly to a food processor. (Don't tell Mildred.) Whizz the mix until it begins to look like breadcrumbs.
3. Slowly add the egg and water and then whizz it further until it forms a ball shape.
4. Remove the dough, and roll out using a flour-dusted rolling pin on a flour-dusted work surface until the pastry is just a little bigger than the size of the tin. Line the tart tin with the pastry, and let the extra pastry hang over the sides of the tin.
5. Chill your pastry tin in the fridge for 30 minutes.
6. While the pastry is chilling, you can make a cup of tea and preheat the oven to 200C/fan 180C/gas 6/350F. Line the tin with nonstick paper and fill with baking beans.
7. Blind bake for 15 minutes in the preheated oven until the pastry turns a lovely pale golden brown.
8. Take out of the oven and remove the baking beans and paper. Carefully trim the excess pastry from

the sides using a sharp knife. Return the empty pastry shell to the oven for another 10-12 minutes or until it is completely dry. Set aside to cool.

9. Reduce the temperature of the oven to 160C/325F. Next measure all the ingredients to make the lemon filling in a bowl and whisk together until smooth. Carefully pour the filling mixture into the cold baked pastry case.

10. Transfer the tart and tray carefully to the oven and bake for 35-40 minutes or until just set but still with a slight wobble in the middle. Don't worry if it rises a little; the filling will sink down a bit when it has cooled.

11. Leave to cool completely and then remove the tarte au citron from the tin and transfer to a serving plate. Finish off with a generous flourish of dusted icing sugar and garnish with a few berries if you like.

Bon appétit!

The best way to keep up with new releases, plus enjoy bonus content and prizes is to join Nancy's newsletter at nancywarren.net

The Great Witches Baking Show

The Great Witches Baking Show - Book 1

Baker's Coven - Book 2

A Rolling Scone - Book 3

The Vampire Knitting Club

When Lucy inherits a knitting shop in Oxford, England, little does she know she's also inheriting a very special knitting circle. These vampires are crazy good knitters (they've had a long time to practice) and they also help solve murders.

Tangles and Treasons - a free prequel for Nancy's newsletter subscribers

The Vampire Knitting Club - Book 1

Stitches and Witches - Book 2

Crochet and Cauldrons - Book 3

Stockings and Spells - Book 4

Purls and Potions - Book 5

Fair Isle and Fortunes - Book 6

Lace and Lies - Book 7

Bobbles and Broomsticks - Book 8

Popcorn and Poltergeists - Book 9

Toni Diamond Mysteries

Toni is a successful saleswoman for Lady Bianca Cosmetics in this series of humorous cozy mysteries. Along with having an eye for beauty and a head for business, Toni's got a nose for trouble and she's never shy about following her instincts, even when they lead to murder.

Frosted Shadow - Book 1

Ultimate Concealer - Book 2

Midnight Shimmer - Book 3

A Diamond Choker For Christmas - A Toni Diamond Mysteries Novella

The Almost Wives Club

An enchanted wedding dress is a matchmaker in this series of romantic comedies where five runaway brides find out who the best men really are!

The Almost Wives Club: Kate - Book 1

Second Hand Bride - Book 2

Bridesmaid for Hire - Book 3

The Wedding Flight - Book 4

If the Dress Fits - Book 5

Take a Chance series

Meet the Chance family, a cobbled together family of eleven kids who are all grown up and finding their ways in life and love.

Kiss a Girl in the Rain - Book 1

Iris in Bloom - Book 2

Blueprint for a Kiss - Book 3

Every Rose - Book 4

Love to Go - Book 5

The Sheriff's Sweet Surrender - Book 6

The Daisy Game - Book 7

Chance Encounter - Prequel

Take a Chance Box Set - Prequel and Books 1-3

For a complete list of books, check out Nancy's website at nancywarren.net

ACKNOWLEDGMENTS

First, I have to thank my mother who taught me to bake and firmly believed that nothing you buy in a bakery or store is ever as good as what you can make at home. I still think she's the best baker in the world. To Gemma Reeves, a great friend and wonderful writer, for all her help on this book. Thanks to my editor Chris and proof reader Judy who make the words run smoothly. Lou Harper at Cover Affairs is my go to cover designer and really brings the vision to life with her witty and wonderful covers. Hollis McCarthy gave voice to these characters in her brilliant narration on the audiobook. Thanks to Cissy Colman for her encouragement and support. Thanks to my great crew of advance readers who still catch typos and give such wonderful feedback. And thanks to every reader who decides to take a chance on my books. I appreciate you all!

ABOUT THE AUTHOR

Nancy Warren is the USA Today Bestselling author of more than 70 novels. She's originally from Vancouver, Canada, though she tends to wander and has lived in England, Italy and California at various times. While living in Oxford she dreamed up The Vampire Knitting Club. She currently splits her time between Bath, UK, where she often pretends she's Jane Austen. Or at least a character in a Jane Austen novel, and Victoria, British Columbia where she enjoys living by the ocean. Favorite moments include being the answer to a crossword puzzle clue in Canada's National Post newspaper, being featured on the front page of the New York Times when her book Speed Dating launched Harlequin's NASCAR series, and being nominated three times for Romance Writers of America's RITA award. She has an MA in Creative Writing from Bath Spa University. She's an avid hiker, loves chocolate and most of all, loves to hear from readers! The best way to stay in touch is to sign up for Nancy's newsletter at www. nancywarren.net.

To learn more about Nancy and her books
www.nancywarren.net

Made in the USA
Coppell, TX
18 April 2021

54063571R10118